donut go breaking my heart

Also by Suzanne Nelson

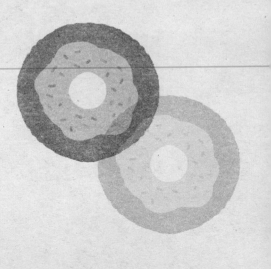

donut go breaking my heart

Suzanne Nelson

SCHOLASTIC INC.

ISBN 978-1-338-04363-1

10 9 8 7 6 5 4   17 18 19 20 21

Printed in the U.S.A.   40
First printing 2017

Book design by Jennifer Rinaldi

For Tyler Beth and Robert James. Welcome
to the world and to our donut-loving family

—S.N.

donut go breaking my heart

Chapter One

Here it comes. The lightning strike of inspiration. The perfect idea. Wait . . . for . . . it.

I stared down at the rows of golden rings, breathing deeply. Their scent was like a sweet, doughy hug in the cramped but cozy kitchen.

Anticipation had kept me warm on the short, snowy walk here from my apartment on Sixth Street in Manhattan's East Village. I'd stayed up past midnight brainstorming without success, but I wasn't worried. One whiff of the fresh-baked goodness from Doughlicious was always enough to set my brain humming.

Helping out at the donut shop was a win-win; it meant I got to spend extra time with my BFF, Kiri Seng, whose parents owned Doughlicious. And my own parents approved. "Work will do her good," my dad had told my mom. "Talking to customers will force her out of her shell."

Well, the work might not have fixed my shyness, since I spent most of the time hiding in the kitchen instead of out front dealing with customers. But I got my best set-design ideas while I kneaded dough or drizzled icing. Last year, while baking donuts, I realized I could rig up a treadmill to create a moving yellow brick road for our school's production of *The Wizard of Oz*.

And now I needed another good idea. It would come. It *had* to come.

I lifted a still-warm donut from the tray and dipped it into a large bowl of caramel. Then I zigzagged melted bittersweet chocolate over the icing and added a sprinkling of sea salt for a finishing touch. I reached for the next donut, and the next after that. The rhythm of the motions had a hypnotic effect, and soon I was lost in thought, envisioning an empty stage, waiting for its perfect set.

A set design showing a fresh, distinctive take on Romeo and Juliet. That was what my application to New York University's summer drama program had asked for. My plan had been to work on the set model over winter break so that I'd be well on my way to finishing it before starting back at school. It was due by February 3. Three weeks from now. I wanted to get into this program *so* badly, more than anything else I'd wanted *ever.* That wanting seemed to be freezing up my brain, because so far, I hadn't come up with a single inspiring thought.

My hands kept moving, dipping in and out of the caramel bowl, but no lightning struck, no ideas came.

"Sheyda!" Mrs. Seng appeared at my elbow, smiling in approval at the now-finished tray of Caramel Dream donuts. "Perfect!"

I smiled back, reluctantly giving up on my quest for inspiration. "Thanks."

She winked. "You're my best icer. I tell Kiri all the time, 'Why can't you ice like Sheyda?' But she says actresses don't do donuts." I stifled a giggle as Mrs. Seng frowned. "My own daughter . . . hating the family business. What am I going to do with that girl?"

"Don't say that, Mrs. Seng. You know Kiri loves you." I patted her shoulder. This was our routine. She groused about Kiri's loathing of all things Doughlicious, and I made her feel better. Mrs. Seng was like my second mom, and the shop was like my second home. My parents, who both worked long hours as lawyers, let me hang out in the shop almost every day after school.

It was an arrangement we'd fallen into back when Kiri and I were barely four. Mom had baked a batch of *latifeh*, my favorite Persian cookie, for our preschool class. Mrs. Seng tasted one of the creamy pistachio cookies and asked Mom for the recipe so she could create a *latifeh*-inspired donut. That got them to talking about family—Mom and Dad's Iranian ancestry and Mrs. Seng's Cambodian background. Soon they were practically in tears reminiscing over the trips they'd made as children to their parents' homelands. They bonded, swapped more recipes, and smiled at how inseparable Kiri and I were on the playground. When Mom mentioned needing to find an afternoon sitter for me, Mrs. Seng wouldn't hear of it. "Sheyda can stay with us," she told Mom. It would be fun for Kiri to have a playmate in the shop, she explained, and keep us both entertained. It had been this way ever since.

"Kiri loves me, yes," mumbled Mrs. Seng now, turning toward the kitchen door with the tray of Caramel Dreams. "But where is the love for the donuts?"

Kiri swung through the kitchen door, rolling her eyes at her mom. Seeing them side by side made me realize how much taller Kiri had grown in the last couple of months. With her long legs and slender frame, Kiri loomed more than a head above her mother, making their face-off almost comical.

"I don't have to love donuts, Mom," Kiri said. "They're nothing but greasy globs of cholesterol. Isn't it enough that I'm here every day making them?"

Mrs. Seng tsked and breezed through the door with her tray. Kiri collapsed against the wall, flicking her short, glossy black hair in annoyance. Over the break she'd cut her hair into a sleek, angled bob, and the new look highlighted her delicate nose and heart-shaped mouth, so that even when she was grimacing, she looked blockbuster-worthy.

"I never thought I'd say this," she groaned, "but winter break *cannot* be over soon enough. If I have to work another full day here, I'll die."

"Please don't." I smiled at Kiri's dramatics. "Who would I eat lunch with at school tomorrow?"

"It could be good for you," Kiri argued, fingering her favorite necklace absently. It had two gold pendants, the comedy and tragedy masks. I'd given it to her for her twelfth birthday, and she'd worn it every day since. "Force you to get up the courage to talk to someone new. Aside from me and Phoebe and Val."

I turned my attention to sifting some powdered sugar onto the next rack of donuts. "I don't need any friends besides you guys." Phoebe and Val finished up our social foursome, but they'd been Kiri's friends before they'd been mine.

"We *are* pretty awesome." Kiri grinned. "I *suppose* we're lucky to have you, too." I tossed an oven mitt at her head, but she deftly ducked. "Okay, okay. I'm just glad our lunches got mixed up in the cubbies in preschool. Otherwise you never would've spoken to me."

I laughed. It was true. Even at age four I'd been a classic wallflower. "Your lunch surprised me, that's all. I'd never seen squid on a stick before." I'd learned to love Mrs. Seng's Cambodian cooking, though, just the way Kiri loved my family's Persian meals.

Kiri sighed. "Speaking of squid, Mrs. Tentacle is at the front counter, waiting for her usual." She clasped her hands together and dropped to her knees. "Would you wait on her today? Spare me her halitosis! Please!"

Mrs. Tentifleur did have the world's worst fish breath (thus the nickname), and I didn't like waiting on her any more than Kiri did. Still, Kiri's ridiculous begging got me laughing until I couldn't help agreeing.

"All right," I said. "But next time, I'm *not* giving in."

Kiri grinned, triumphant. This was how our friendship worked. We had an unspoken queen bee–sidekick pact. Kiri could talk her way out of or into anything using her performer's charm. Most people, including me, found it a quality more loveable than bossy. Besides, Kiri's boldness made me feel braver. If it wasn't for Kiri, I doubt my social circle would ever have grown beyond my parents and older sister, Mina. Neither one of us was über popular, but Kiri's infectious energy gave her the ability to float around every group at school without ever settling on one. And because I was her tagalong, her friends always became mine. I didn't mind. I was grateful to stay behind the scenes. That was what I did best.

I pushed through the door into the shop, with its buttercream walls and lemon-yellow café tables and chairs. I glanced in dread at the counter. To my relief, I discovered that Mrs. Tentifleur was already seated at a table with her cappuccino and Blackberry Bliss donut.

"Can you help whoever comes in next, Sheyda?" Mrs. Seng

asked me, hurrying toward the kitchen. "I've got to finish the Nutty Professors."

I nodded, my mouth watering at the mention of Mrs. Seng's latest creation—a chocolate donut filled with peanut butter, glazed with honey icing, and sprinkled with candied almond slivers. I'd have to grab one to snack on later.

I snapped out of my donut daydream when the bell on the shop door jingled. I'd been prepared to help a customer, but the person that walked into the store was more Abominable Snowman than human. A bulky, fur-lined parka stood before me, the hood pulled so low around aviator sunglasses that I could only make out the slightest hint of a boy's face.

The boy didn't approach the counter but hung back, looking at the glass display cases through his mirrored shades. I was just about to greet him when three adults blew into the shop, bringing a swirl of snowflakes in with them. These three were almost as heavily bundled, and one of the men burst out with, "People! Tell me. Is my nose still attached to my face, or has it frozen off?"

"This is our last stop, Simeon," a woman in treacherously high-heeled boots said impatiently. "Quit whining."

"Good," Simeon mumbled. "There's a sunlamp with my name on it back at the hotel."

The boy in sunglasses turned to the three of them. "Can we get this over with?" he snapped. "We've seen a dozen of these dumps already. Just . . . pick one!"

Dumps? I stiffened. How dare he! At his outburst, the other three huddled around him protectively, whispering things like "give it a try" and "we'll make do." After a minute, the boy abruptly nodded to the others, then headed straight for me.

"We'll take a dozen to go." His voice was clipped and tense, and I squirmed. How awkward to be staring at my own reflection in his glasses and not be able to see the expression in his eyes! My heart sped nervously.

"Um, sure. What kind would you like?" I asked.

He shrugged and tossed two twenties onto the counter. "Whatever. Doesn't matter."

I scowled, annoyed at his attitude. Didn't he realize these donuts were works of art? Eager to get this exchange over with, I hurriedly selected a random dozen and put them in a box.

"Here you go." I held out the box, but as he took it, the bottom opened up, pouring donuts all down his parka.

He stared at the mess of icing and powdered sugar covering his front.

"Look what you did!" he cried.

"Oh my gosh, I'm so sorry." I rushed around the counter with a pile of napkins. "I must've accidentally had the box upside down. Here, let me help—"

"Accidentally?" he grumbled. "Right. I've heard that one before." I wiped some of the icing off his parka, but he stepped back, grabbing the napkins out of my hand. "Stop. That's only making it worse."

He was right. The icing was smearing a bigger swath across his coat. "Sorry," I said. "I'll get you a wet rag from the back . . ."

"Forget it." He crushed the napkins into a ball and stomped

toward the door. "I'm out of here," he called to his companions, then shoved the door open with such force that it slammed against the front window with a clang.

I cringed. Three pairs of eyes turned toward me, as if awaiting explanation.

"I didn't mean to—" I began.

The woman stepped forward, her sleek red ponytail curling around one side of her earmuffs. "Don't pay him any mind," she said. "He's tense today, that's all." She stuck out a confident gloved hand, which I shook tentatively. "I'm Jillian Yens, film director at Everest Movie Studio."

I blinked. Movie studio? Huh?

Jillian continued. "This is Simeon Dashan, our casting agent, and Gerard Perdue, our location scout." Simeon offered a small bow and Gerard a salute. "We called earlier and spoke with Mrs. Seng? We're in New York for the filming of Cabe Sadler's newest romantic comedy, *Donut Go Breaking My Heart*."

No sooner had the words "Cabe Sadler" escaped Jillian's lips than Kiri burst through the kitchen door.

"Did I just hear the name Cabe Sadler?" Kiri asked, her voice three octaves higher than usual.

Jillian nodded. "You did."

Oh boy, I thought, mentally prepping myself. And three, two, one . . .

"Cabe Sadler!" Kiri shrieked, grabbing my hands and jumping up and down. "He's incredible. I mean, I don't really worship him or anything, but . . ." She sighed, visibly quivering with joy. "He's the most perfect human being ever born."

"Well. How . . . nice." Jillian glanced back at Simeon and Gerard with an expression that clearly said, *Another fanatic.*

To say that Cabe was Kiri's celebrity obsession was an understatement. There wasn't an inch of wall space in her bedroom that wasn't plastered with his movie posters or magazine cutouts. Kiri followed him on every social media platform known to mankind. Sure, Cabe was cute, but I'd seen his face so many hundreds of times that I didn't even think twice about it anymore. I'd grown a Cabe-immunity.

Kiri stared at Jillian with awe. "Do you actually *know* him?"

"Y-yes," came Jillian's hesitant reply, followed by another shriek from Kiri. Jillian peered around Kiri, giving me a pleading glance. "Might we speak with Mrs. Seng?" the director asked. "We're interested in using Doughlicious as the central location for the film shoot, and I'd like to discuss details and compensation."

This time, Kiri's shriek was deafening.

"I'll get her," I said, and Jillian gave me a grateful nod. As I slipped into the kitchen, I could hear Kiri drilling Jillian, Simeon, and Gerard with questions about the script and casting calls. When I returned with Mrs. Seng, Kiri was still going.

"You know, I played Dorothy in our middle school's production of *The Wizard of Oz* last spring," Kiri was rambling, "*and* Sandy in *Grease* in October. My drama teacher says I have real talent, and I already have so much experience—"

"Mrs. Seng?" Jillian said with obvious relief, then sidestepped Kiri to fill Mrs. Seng in on everything.

Kiri turned to me, her cheeks flushed with excitement. "Omigod. Can you believe this is happening? It's unreal. They're holding a casting call for a small role tomorrow afternoon, and Simeon says it's an open audition for girls ages eleven to fourteen." Her smile spread. "This could be a real shot for me, don't you think? My chance at Hollywood!"

"It's amazing," I said, squeezing her arm affectionately. Kiri had always wanted to be an actress. I'd watched every one of her performances, and she was a natural, stepping into roles so thoroughly that, sometimes, her characters' mannerisms and personalities became hers temporarily offstage, too. She'd wanted her Sandy to have a Southern accent, so for weeks before the curtain went up on *Grease*, Kiri perfected her "y'alls." It was so convincing that one Doughlicious customer had asked what town in Georgia she was from.

Kiri had been trying to persuade her parents to move to Los Angeles for years in hopes that living there might up her chances of being "discovered." Mr. and Mrs. Seng wouldn't consider it, but that didn't stop Kiri from pleading with them regularly.

"Will you come to my audition with me?" she asked me now.

"Um . . ." I waffled, my stomach tightening. Tomorrow after

school I was supposed to have a meeting with our drama club teacher, Ms. Feld, to talk about my *Romeo and Juliet* set model. Winter was a downtime in the club; we were in between our fall and spring productions, which meant Ms. Feld's schedule was more open right now. When she was younger, Ms. Feld had been in a few Broadway plays, and I thought she might be able to give me some pointers on stage logistics. "The thing is, I have my meeting with Ms. Feld and—"

"Ooooh, what will I wear?" Kiri interrupted. "I've got to make some tea with honey right now. Doesn't my voice still sound a little raspy from that cold I had last week? It has to be silky smooth tomorrow . . ." She glanced at me, and I could see what I'd said finally registering with her. "Ms. Feld? Oh, she'll understand if you reschedule. Sheyda, please come with me. I'd totally freak without you there. You know I'd do the same for you."

I took a deep breath, my *no* all ready, but then it got stuck in my throat. I knew she wouldn't really freak, but I also liked that she wanted me there with her. I liked feeling needed. And, Kiri *would've* done the same for me. Of course, I'd never audition for anything involving a stage, camera, or any kind of audience, so it was sort of a moot point. "Okay, okay, I'll go." I smiled as she threw her arms around me.

"Yes! Thank you, thank you!"

"But"—I held up a finger—"that means I have to go home now so I can make some headway on my application. That way, when I *do* meet with Ms. Feld, I'll actually have something to show her."

"Sure, okay, that's fine," Kiri said. "I'll tell Mom you had to go. How is the set coming anyway?"

"It's not," I said as I grabbed my coat, hat, and messenger bag from underneath the counter. "I just hope I don't have designer's block."

"You? Never!" Kiri's eyes softened in sympathy. "You'll figure it out. Don't panic."

Mrs. Seng was still talking with Jillian, Simeon, and Gerard about filming logistics, so I waved to them as Kiri walked me to the front door. I pushed it open and stopped.

A limo was parked in front of the store. Through its open

window, I caught a glimpse of the boy who'd been in the shop before. His sunglasses mirrored the drifting snowflakes, and the hood of his parka was pushed back, revealing a shock of messy blond hair. His mouth was drawn tight.

"Still copping the attitude, huh?" I mumbled, then turned to Kiri. "That guy came in with the rest of the movie people. I know I dumped donuts on him, but he doesn't have to give me a death glare." Kiri was staring, her mouth gaping. "Kiri? Earth to Kiri?"

Kiri's eyes didn't move from the limo. "I'd recognize that glorious mane of hair anywhere. Don't you know who he is?" she squealed. *"That's Cabe Sadler!"*

I looked back to the limo. There was a brief flash of aquamarine eyes, shadeless now, meeting mine. His eyes surprised me. They seemed hard *and* soft all at once, like they were robins' eggs sheltering something sweet and vulnerable inside. My heart gave a funny leap, and then the limo's dark window rolled up.

"Wait." Kiri frowned. "Did you say you dumped donuts on him?" I gave an innocent shrug, and before she had time to become properly horrified by the idea, I scooted away.

"Call you later!" I said with a wave. Then I pulled on my hat, forcing myself to focus on the sidewalk as I hurried past the limo. I wasn't about to give Cabe Sadler the satisfaction of thinking I was gawking at him. Not for a second.

I recognized the familiar fragrance of dinner as soon as I entered my building. *Khoresh Fesenjan*—chicken and pomegranate stew. *Yum.* It was a dish whose aroma wafted from our third-floor walk-up apartment all the way to the downstairs foyer. Our neighbors didn't mind. In fact, they loved taking leftovers whenever we had them. Our building was small, and it was home to our family, a family from Soweto, South Africa, one from Moscow, and a couple from Caracas, Venezuela. We all happily embraced one another's cooking; in a building as compact as ours, it would've been tough to avoid it. I smiled now, thinking about the delicious meal ahead. Maybe before dinner I could steal some alone time to work on my application.

I heard the tense voices echoing into the stairwell as I reached our landing. I sighed and stuck the key in our door. So much for peace and quiet. They were at it again.

"You are the strictest parents on the planet!" my older sister, Mina, cried as I stepped into the narrow hallway off the kitchen.

When it wasn't loud with fighting, I loved our apartment. It was the apartment that *Mâdarbozorg*, my grandma, had moved into when she'd emigrated from Iran as a young woman. The apartment where she and my grandpa had married and raised my mother. It was still decorated with their things: a crimson couch, hand-woven Persian rugs, ornate lanterns, and cinnamon-colored walls. Dad's parents lived in Florida, first generation Persian Americans, and we visited them a few times a year (I loved seeing them, even if Grandpa still pinched my cheek and declared, "*Moosh bokhoratet*," which means, "A mouse could eat you!" It was Grandpa's way of saying "cute" in Farsi, and I was so glad no one outside my family knew the literal translation.) Yes, I loved my dad's family, but Mom's parents' had died before I was born. Living here made me feel like I knew a part of them, their tastes, the family photos that they'd loved, the books they'd read. I wondered what they would make of the yelling echoing off the walls of their home right now.

I hung up my coat, then tiptoed toward my bedroom, but Mina's eyes lasered in on me. "Sheyda, will you back me up on this? Tell them how ridiculous they're being."

I blinked. No way was I getting dragged into an argument between Mina and my parents. "Um, I don't have a clue what you're talking about."

Mina threw up her hands, her flushed cheeks matching the neon-red streak in her pixie-cut hair. "Doesn't anyone in this family ever hear a word I say?" She slumped down in her chair at the kitchen table, then glared at me. "The ski trip to Vermont with Rehann and Josh? Remember?"

"Oh . . . that."

Mina had been whispering about the trip to me for weeks, plotting ways to convince Mom and Dad to let her go. Rehann was Mina's best friend, and Josh was Mina's latest crush at East Village High. It was Rehann who'd had the idea for a ski trip, since her parents owned a condo in Vermont. I'd watched Mina's fantasy blossoming as she gleefully texted Rehann and Josh, making plans to go the first weekend in February. The whole time I knew that her chance of going on the trip was as low as the chance that New Yorkers would give up bagels.

Now I could see the vein on the side of Dad's temple pulsing, and Mom was wearing her classic disapproval face. I didn't like seeing them stressed, but Mina had this effect on them. She'd been dealt the rebel card from birth. The list of her "achievements" had grown into a kind of legend in the Nazari family. At age three she'd poured dishwashing detergent into her preschool's toilets to give bubble baths to the classroom's dolls. At age five she'd tried "running away" to live in Tompkins Square Park. Luckily, Mr. Giovanni, the owner of the corner bodega, caught sight of her toting her pillow and backpack before she could even cross Sixth Street. Last year, she'd cut off her beautiful long locks before dyeing the remaining jagged hair red. The last few months, she'd taken her renegade act up a notch.

"You're not going," Dad said firmly to Mina. "That's the end of it."

"But Rehann's and Josh's parents will all go as chaperones! I'll be safer on the slopes of Killington than I am riding the subway! You can't say no!" She jabbed a finger at me, and I pressed my back against the wall, wanting to disappear. "Sheyda, tell them! You think I should be able to go, don't you?"

Mom glanced at me, her eyes sending me a silent, *Please don't.* Ugh. I hated it when Mina put me in the middle.

"I have some work to do," I muttered, then hurried down the hall.

"Way to throw me under the bus!" Mina called after me. As I shut the bedroom door, I heard the arguing resume. I wished I was back at Doughlicious. It was impossible to think straight while listening to angry voices.

I'd only just finished setting up my set-building materials on the desk when I heard the front door slam. A minute later, Mom stuck her head into my bedroom, looking like she'd just escaped combat.

"Was that Mina leaving?" I asked.

She sighed. "She went for a run." She pressed her forehead against the doorframe, closing her eyes. "I *hate* being the enemy."

"You're not, Mom," I said, getting up to give her a quick hug.

She surveyed the desk. "Working on your application?" she asked, and before I could answer she added absently, "Looks great."

I glanced at the blank sketch pad. Sure. It looked great. Like a great, big nothing.

Mom turned toward the kitchen. "I'm going to finish up dinner. Too bad this isn't our takeout night."

"I know, but it smells great." Living in the city wasn't cheap, especially on Mom and Dad's salaries (they were both pro bono lawyers). We were always careful with money, so our family rule was takeout once a month. "I can help with dinner," I offered, hoping to cheer her up.

Mom hesitated. "Don't you have work to do?"

"It can wait," I said. I took one last look at my desk, my stomach sinking. I'd get back to work later.

But if I didn't come up with an idea by February, what was I going to do?

Chapter Two

The next morning, what was left of yesterday's snow had turned gray with city soot. I skirted the slushy piles on my walk to school. East Village Middle School was only four blocks from our apartment building, and thankfully Kiri's building was on the way.

Kiri was waiting for me on her stoop, as usual. I gaped at her bulging tote bag. Its weight, in combination with her backpack, was making her list to one side.

"What's that for?" I asked as she fell into step beside me.

"Potential outfits for the audition," Kiri said. "I need your help deciding what to wear. I have to make just the right impression." She held her mittened hand aloft, like a Shakespearean performer poised to recite a soliloquy. "Every great actress has an unforgettable presence. She leaves it like a fragrance, even after she's left the stage." I laughed, and Kiri raised a scolding eyebrow. "You're mocking me. Fine. Be that way. You can't possibly understand the suffering of an aspiring actress."

"What about the suffering of an aspiring set designer, huh?" I peered at the mock seriousness of her face, then elbowed her as we cracked up. "Well. No one could ever doubt your flair for the dramatic. And of course I'll help you pick an outfit, even though you look glam no matter what."

"Aw . . ." She tipped her head against mine in a BFF cuddle, then stopped, staring ahead.

"Kiri?" I followed her gaze.

A swarm of camera-wielding press crowded around our school. News vans were lined up in the street, surrounding a limo.

I gasped. "Wow. What's with the paparazzi?"

"I don't know." Kiri's whisper was high with excitement. "It's gotta be good. Come on, before we miss something!" Kiri ducked and shoved us through arms and cameras until Principal Gomez appeared before us, holding up his palms as a barrier to the crowd.

"Please," he told the reporters. He ushered me and Kiri up the school steps to join dozens of other lingering, curious kids. "This is an educational establishment. Students have to be able to get in the door."

Suddenly, a commotion rose up from the kids on the steps. One girl shrieked, "Omigod, it's him! Cabe Sadler!"

There was Cabe, fighting his way out of the limo alongside people I guessed might either be his bodyguards or his parents. There was something tender and protective about the way the woman wrapped her arm around him, so I was leaning toward parents. Today Cabe wore a camel-colored leather blazer, a cream V-neck sweater, and torn jeans. He looked every part the trendy celeb, and I couldn't stop myself from staring (just a little). He *was* cute. Cuter even than he was in photos. There was something off in his expression, though. His smile was too tight, his eyes holding a hint of exasperation.

Of course, I thought. *He thinks he's above his adoring fans.*

He gave a brief wave to the press before his parents whisked him through the school doors and out of sight.

"All of you inside before the bell sounds," Principal Gomez ordered. "I won't excuse a single tardy for this racket."

There was a rush for the door. Everyone was fighting for a good view of Cabe walking down the hall. Kiri and I were crushed into the mix, but by the time we wrenched free, Cabe was gone.

"Darn it." Kiri's face fell. "I wanted to say hi. He might need help finding his classes, or opening his locker, or—"

"He's filming a movie at your donut shop." I offered her a calming smile. "You're going to see him again. Promise." I glanced at my watch. "We've got to get to class."

Kiri gave one longing look down the hallway, sighed, and then turned toward the stairs.

"See you at lunch," I called after her. As I passed the main office window, I saw Cabe and his parents filling out paper-work at the counter. Cabe lifted his head and our eyes met. Surprise flickered across his features, then annoyance. He'd recognized me, and one thing was obvious: He wasn't happy to see me.

When Principal Gomez gave the morning announcements, he made a special speech about respecting Cabe's privacy. About being friendly to him but treating him like any other run-of-the-mill new student. Yeah . . . right.

In the hallways, mobs of kids rushed to wherever Cabe was, following him to his locker, his classes, even to the bathroom (at least none of the girls actually went in!). Most of the boys seemed to be jostling for dibs on Cabe's friendship, while the girls were either starstruck, crushing, or both. I overheard Trinity, the most popular girl in school, whispering to her besties, "He's so delish. Heath better step it up a notch, or Cabe might give him some competition." Heath was Trinity's boyfriend, but it wasn't hard to imagine Trinity dumping him for a celeb of Cabe's magnitude.

Cabe acted polite, giving out autographs to everyone who asked. Still, he was aloof, tucking his head deeper into the collar of his jacket and avoiding direct eye contact.

By the time the bell rang for lunch, I was sick of being jostled around by stampeding kids dying to take selfies with our resident celeb. Our school was feeling uncomfortably claustrophobic. So I headed for my special hiding spot.

As soon as I stepped into the dimly lit auditorium, my breathing slowed. Thanks to donations from alumni, our auditorium was a proper theater with tiered rows of cushioned seats, state-of-the-art acoustics, and a Broadway-sized stage.

I headed down the aisle and onto the stage, then dipped into the left wing, enjoying the cool quiet. I stuck my head into Ms. Feld's office, which she'd converted from a one-time dressing room. She was at her computer, and notes from an opera aria wafted through the air.

She gave me a smile. "Come for a breather, *bubala?*"

I nodded. Ms. Feld got that about me. That sometimes I needed to escape the loudness and chaos of the school day. "It's crazy out there."

"I heard." She waved her hand. "Between you and me, I'm not entirely certain his talent lives up to the hype." I giggled as she pressed a conspiring finger to her lips. "Are you coming by after school to chat about your application?"

My heart sank. "Oh, I'm so sorry, but can we do it another day?" I explained about Kiri's audition. "I really don't want to postpone, but—"

"Of course you should go with Kiri. The application can wait. Knowing you, you'll have it done long before the deadline anyway. You've never let me down before." She smiled. "I still remember when that enormous hair dryer broke halfway through the opening night of *Grease*. I feared the 'Beauty School Dropout' song would be a disaster, and then you came in with—"

"—the janitor's floor fan." I grinned, remembering.

"Brilliant improv." Ms. Feld applauded me. "So. We can meet next Monday morning, before school. Yes?" I nodded, and she shooed me away. "Go on then. Before you run out of time."

I waved, then climbed the stairs up to the catwalk far above the stage. I loved to sit up here. Ms. Feld was the only one who knew my secret. She'd discovered my hiding spot last year. I'd thought she'd lecture me on safety or something, but she never did. Instead, she told me I could visit the catwalk whenever I needed to, as long as I checked in with her first.

When the drama club put on its shows, I had the advantage of seeing the sets with a hawk's-eye view. And it was peaceful up above—a world of its own where I could just "be" without anyone expecting me to speak or be spoken to. It was basically a shy person's heaven.

I took a few steps along the dark catwalk, using my cell phone's flashlight for guidance. Just as I was about to sit down, a shadow moved on the other end of the walk. My heart jumped.

"Who's there?" I called.

The shadow took a few steps in my direction, and my flashlight illuminated Cabe's face.

"What are you doing here?" he asked.

My cheeks blazed with anger. "What do you mean? This is my—" I was about to say "hiding spot" but caught myself. That could sound babyish, and besides, why should I tell him that, when he'd likely just smirk? "I work on sets for drama club, so . . ." My voice died as I registered the disinterest on his face. "Never mind," I mumbled.

"I didn't think anyone else would be up here," he said flatly.

"No one usually is." I stiffened. Of all the people to trespass on my secret spot, it had to be *him*.

His gaze swept the sea of empty seats beyond the stage. "It's so small. No legroom in the rows."

"It's New York. No theater here has legroom."

"Huh. It's not Shrine Auditorium. That's for sure."

I frowned. "I guess not," I snapped, "but since we're not planning on hosting the Oscars, we're happy with it." I made a show of checking the time on my phone. "I'm, uh, I should go—"

"No!" Cabe's voice echoed louder across the stage than we both expected, and I jumped a little. "Look, if you're going to snap a pic of me, a heads-up would be cool . . ."

"What?" I asked blankly. "I wasn't—"

"Your phone," he interrupted. "Weren't you just using the camera?"

"Um . . . no," I stammered.

"Sure you weren't." Cabe's sarcasm stunned me. "Just like you didn't dump those donuts on me on purpose."

"What are you *talking* about?"

He scoffed. "Fans get crazy. You'll do anything to get my attention or start some trend on Instagram. You probably followed me in here."

He wasn't just being rude. He was being *obnoxiously* rude. I wanted to tell him exactly what I thought, but when it came to confrontation, I was like the Cowardly Lion, tongue-tied with my tail tucked between my legs. My heart pounded out what I wanted to say, but try as I might, no words would come.

Then Cabe's cell lit up in his hand. He glanced at the screen, and in its blue glow his expression hardened. "My manager," he said abruptly. "He's probably calling about the premiere of *Very Valentine*. So let me just beat you to the punch. It's hitting theaters Valentine's weekend and they're doing the big premiere here in Manhattan. There'll be plenty of photo ops. Go ahead, tell all your friends."

He turned to leave, answering his cell. He didn't bother looking back. His shadow was already melding into the staircase.

I stood there for a minute shaking with fury. I didn't care how much Kiri gushed about Cabe Sadler. He might be okay at acting like a nice guy on-screen, but that was all it would ever be. One big, enormous act.

"Where were you?" Kiri asked when I got to the cafeteria. She was sitting with Phoebe and Val. "We finished eating ages ago, and you promised you'd help me with outfits for the audition."

"Sorry." I was on the verge of telling her that I ran into Cabe, but instinct told me not to. Cabe's snob routine had already soured my mood, and rehashing it would only make it worse. "I had to tell Ms. Feld about canceling our meeting and it took longer than I thought it would."

"Like the whole lunch period!" Kiri cried. Then her expression softened. "It's okay. Phoebe helped me decide on the clothes."

"No small task, let me tell you." Phoebe groaned, redoing her tangled auburn topknot. Phoebe was one of the lighting techs for drama club, and the combat boots she wore every day were the perfect symbol of her no-nonsense persona. She had a dry, sometimes cutting sense of humor that I loved, mostly because her jokes were never directed at me.

Val, the cheeriest of our bunch with her glee club voice and Disney princess optimism, giggled.

"Hey. Fifteen minutes to pick an outfit is fast for me!" Kiri said. "Besides"—she grinned at me—"nothing could put me in a bad mood today."

"Why? What happened?"

"Kiri's the luckiest girl in our entire school, that's what!" Val cried, her tone tinged with jealousy. "Cabe Sadler's in her history class!"

"That's not all, either." Kiri smiled into her can of seltzer. "Mr. Tambe made us partners for the Famous People from History project." Kiri gripped my hand, her eyes huge with excitement. "I'm going to spend so much time with him working on it! And if I get the part in *Donut Go Breaking My Heart*, I'll see him even more!"

"That's great," I said, wanting to be genuinely happy for her. Instead, I wondered how much more Cabe-mania I'd have to deal with now. I took a deep breath. Before Kiri totally fell in love with Cabe, shouldn't I warn her what he was really like? "But, Kiri—"

"Oh no." Kiri's smile sagged. "You're starting with your 'buts.' That's never good." Kiri was always telling me that I burst her bubbles with all my hesitating and but-ing. "Can't you just be happy for me?"

Phoebe gave me an acerbic glance. "Be happy for her,

Sheyda, so she'll quit talking about him. Please. For my sake, at least."

I laughed. "Okay. Just be careful, that's all. I have a feeling the real-life Cabe is different from the big-screen one."

"You did it anyway. You pulled an Eeyore." Kiri dropped her forehead to the table while Val shot me a scolding look. Then Kiri's head sprang back up, her eyes bright. "You know what? You're right. He *is* going to be different in real life. He's going to be even better."

A few hours later, Mrs. Seng, Kiri, and I stepped out of the elevator at the Soho Grand Hotel. The auditions were being held in a suite on the top floor, and the poshness of the suite's foyer alone was enough to give me the jitters. People scurried around with cameras, piles of clothing, and lighting equipment while we watched in amazement.

"It's fantastic, isn't it?" Kiri said.

Nerve-racking was more like it.

A frazzled-looking assistant balancing two trays of coffees ushered us into a sitting room where a dozen other girls waited to audition. Within minutes, Simeon breezed in, greeting everyone by handing out copies of the script.

"Here's what you need to know about this movie," he said. "Cabe plays Prince Dalton of a fictional European country named Atlantia. Fed up with his royal duties, he runs away to Manhattan and poses as a commoner. He takes a job at a donut shop. A series of hilarious mishaps ensue as Prince Dalton falls for his love interest, Tia. Eventually he has to reveal his true identity and return to royal life, having grown sager and kinder, yada yada . . . and henceforth everyone lives in eternal bliss. Got it?"

There were nods, and Simeon gave a golf-clap. "Good. Now. You'll be auditioning for the part of Tia's cousin Marie—a savvy but shy girl who's the key to revealing Prince Dalton's true identity to Tia. She works at Doughlicious with Dalton, and she instantly notices that something about him is amiss." He scanned the room. "You'll be reading from page fifty of the script. Take a few minutes to study the lines before we call you in."

Kiri pored over the lines. "Should I read my lines in a snarky way? What do you think?"

"Just read it like yourself," I suggested, not having a clue if that was sound advice or not.

Mrs. Seng harrumphed beside us. "Foolishness. Why I agreed to bring you here is beyond me."

"Don't be grumpy, Mrs. Seng," I said. I pulled a slip of paper from my pocket and handed it to her. "I found a new donut recipe for us to try. Raspberry-Cheesecake Surprise. We could tweak it by adding a lemon glaze on top."

"Thanks, Sheyda." She gave me a grateful look. "At least *your* head is in the right place."

"Mom—" Kiri started, but then the director's assistant called her name. Kiri instantly pulled me from my chair, too. "You're coming with me," she hissed. Before I could protest, Kiri dragged me through the door into the much larger audition room.

There was an open space in the middle, where an *X* was marked in blue duct tape on the floor. Jillian, Simeon, and Gerard—the threesome I'd met at Doughlicious—were all seated on the couches with tablets and coffees in hand. There were several other people I didn't recognize, but I assumed they also worked for Everest Movie Studio.

My stomach flipped. Cabe was here, too, slouched in an armchair. He didn't even look up from his phone. Nothing about his demeanor said that he wanted to be at these auditions or that he was even paying attention.

"I'm sorry, but we can only audition you one at a time," Jillian said, nodding toward me.

"Oh no!" My cheeks flamed, and Cabe's eyes shot up. "I'm, um, here for moral support."

Jillian glanced at Cabe, as if awaiting approval. He frowned and gave a single nod.

"You can stay," Jillian said to me.

Well, well, somebody's got some serious pull around here, I thought. I pressed my back against the wall, trying to fade into the background, while Kiri beamed, awaiting instructions.

"Okay, Kiri," Simeon said. "Stand on that mark on the floor.

We'll take some quick headshots for our records, and then Cabe will join you for the reading."

"I'm going to read with him? Great! Really great!" Kiri flung her hair and jutted out her hip like she was posing.

"Thanks," Simeon said after Kiri had batted her eyelashes and pursed her lips for the camera. "Cabe, we're ready for you now." No response. "Cabe?"

"Yup." Cabe took his time setting down his phone. He moved to Kiri's side, then added to Simeon, "Let's get this over with."

Irritation broiled inside me. Cabe could at least be polite, even if he *was* bored.

"Kiri, you can start from the top of the page," Simeon instructed. "Whenever you're ready."

Kiri nodded and began reading. "Listen, Dalton. I saw the way you looked at Tia just now. Something's up."

Cabe recited the lines from memory. "I don't know what you're talking about," he said, crinkling his brow in confusion.

"Come on." Kiri leaned toward him. She laid a hand on his arm. "You can tell me. I want to keep your secrets—"

"Stop!" Jillian said, checking the script. "Kiri, it's actually 'I can keep a secret.'"

Kiri giggled. "Oops. Can we start over?"

"One more time," Jillian said. "And maybe don't touch his arm. Remember. You're Tia's cousin. You don't have the crush on Prince Dalton. Tia does."

Kiri nodded and tried again. But I could see what Jillian meant. Kiri was coming off like she was flirting with Cabe (and my guess was that she *was*). After a few more minutes, Jillian held up her hand.

"Thank you, Kiri. We've got what we need."

Kiri gave me a triumphant thumbs-up and sailed out of the room. I started for the door, but my foot caught on a cord and sent a lighting stand crashing to the floor.

"Omigod, I'm so sorry," I gushed, scrambling to right the light.

"Don't worry about it," Simeon said, but Cabe was already beside me, picking up the light.

"Just leave it," he grumbled. What he really meant, though, was "leave."

I straightened, feeling something inside me snap. I'd had enough, and the words poured out before I could stop them. "Just so you know, that wasn't on purpose. And neither were the donuts yesterday or anything else you think I've done to you." *Omigod, what am I doing?* the inner me screamed, *Shut up!* The outer me wasn't listening, though. She kept right on going. "I'm a klutz, okay? That's all. I don't have some hidden agenda to sabotage you on social media. You may have legions of fans, but I'm *not* one of them!"

I couldn't be sure, but the shock in Cabe's eyes looked genuine. For the first time since I'd met him, he seemed to be at a complete loss.

Then I noticed the silence. Everyone in the room was frozen in place, mouths half-open, possibly afraid to so much as breathe. The reality of what I'd done dawned on me. I'd just told off Cabe Sadler in front of all these important film people. Not only that, but I'd probably just destroyed any chance Kiri had of getting the part. Oh. Crud.

I glanced at the door. Kiri had already gone outside and missed the whole freak-out. "Um . . . sorry for the interruption everybody," I stammered. "And just so you know, Kiri's really talented. She was terrific, wasn't she? Not anything like, um, me. She and Cabe would work well together." More silence. "So don't let this impact your decision about her, okay?" I paused, twisting my hands together nervously.

Cabe opened his mouth, seemingly on the verge of saying something. Then he stopped, glancing at Simeon and the others.

Simeon had this odd expression on his face that completely threw me. Why didn't he look mad? Why was everyone staring at me but not calling security to have me removed from the building? Beyond flustered, I mumbled a hurried good-bye and scooted out of the room.

Kiri was waiting for me, dying to know what I thought of her audition. I told her she was a natural. I didn't tell her about my mega meltdown. If I'd blown her chances, she'd find out soon enough.

Kiri was still talking about the audition two hours later, during the late afternoon rush at Doughlicious. Business always picked up between four and six on weekdays. A lot of desperate nannies and parents brought kids in for snacks, and then there were the office workers who had to have their afternoon latte and donut.

I was trying to remain upbeat, but reassuring Kiri that she was brilliantly talented was getting the teensiest bit tiresome. Still, she was always my biggest cheerleader when it came to my set design ideas. She'd be doing the same for me right now if *I* was the one in need of some confidence boosting. It was what best friends did.

I was just handing the last three S'mores donuts to a frazzled au pair when Simeon walked into the shop. I elbowed Kiri.

"Look who's here," I whispered. "Probably to tell you that you got the part!"

"Omigod! How do I look?" She did a little feet-only happy dance behind the counter, where no one else could see. Then she coolly waved to Simeon.

He gave a small bow. "Ladies."

I held my breath, and beside me, sensed Kiri doing the same. Simeon's eyes settled on me.

"Sheyda, do you have a second to talk?"

I shot a confused look at Kiri, who looked equally bewildered.

"Um, is this about the light I knocked over?" I asked Simeon. "If it's broken, I—"

"No, no, nothing like that." Simeon grinned at me. "I've been sent here . . . to offer you the part of Marie in the movie."

I blinked, dumbfounded, and shook my head. "I'm sorry. I'm not sure what you mean."

"The role of Tia's cousin. Marie? You were just at the audition a few hours ago?" He tapped his foot impatiently as he waited for this to sink in.

The audition? My heart slammed into my throat. "But," I

sputtered, "I didn't audition. Kiri did." I gave Kiri a pleading look, but she was staring, pale-faced.

Simeon nodded gently at Kiri. "I'm sorry," he said to her. "We all agreed that your audition had promise. *If* the role were for Dalton's love interest. But that's not the slant we're looking for this time."

"Oh!" Kiri blushed. "His love interest," she repeated, and I could almost see the wheels in her head whirring with renewed hope. "Well, that's at least something, isn't it?"

"It's great!" I said. "And now that you know what they liked . . ."

"I can perfect my onscreen persona!" Kiri finished.

Simeon turned back to me. "The rest of the auditions were canceled. It seems you're the first and *only* choice."

My stomach knotted. My thoughts reeled. I sank into the nearest chair, speechless, as Kiri burst out laughing.

"This is a joke, right?" Kiri said to Simeon. She glanced at me, probably expecting me to shout, "Gotcha!"

"I—I . . ." I glanced at Simeon in desperation. This *had* to be a fluke.

"Not a joke," Simeon confirmed.

"But Sheyda doesn't act!" Kiri blurted. The good-sport grin she'd been wearing sank into disappointment. "She'd freeze up the second you put her in front of the camera."

I bristled, feeling a jolt of defensiveness. It was true; my greatest fear was being in the spotlight, whether that meant being called on in class or giving oral presentations. Still. It was the way Kiri said it, like it was an absurd idea, me acting. A small part of me wished I could prove her wrong.

"Well, I saw *something* in that audition room when you were talking to Cabe," Simeon said to me matter-of-factly. "That's exactly the sort of charmingly witty feel we're going for with Marie."

I thought back to my outburst with Cabe. "The thing is," I began quietly, "I'm not normally so . . . outspoken. I'm more of a behind-the-scenes girl."

"Your protests are falling on deaf ears." Simeon tilted his head, his shrewd gaze assessing me. "Besides, you have those fabulous big, dark eyes. *Made* for the big screen."

I blushed. "I don't—"

"And here's the big perk," Simeon said. He leaned close and told me the amount the studio would pay me for playing Marie.

The number stopped me cold. It wasn't enough to pay the entire tuition for the summer drama program, but it would cover the application fee plus supplies for my design model. Whatever I had left over I could give to my parents to put toward the tuition. Could I really pass up this offer if it would take some stress off Mom and Dad?

I glanced at Kiri, and it was as if she'd been reading my mind. The disappointment on her face had given way to a struggling but supportive smile. She pulled me aside. "Take the part," she said definitively. "This is a no-brainer. Think of what you could do with the money."

"I know. But . . . what about you? This is your dream role. I can't take it from you—"

"You heard Simeon. I'm not going to get the part anyway. Besides, now I can live vicariously through you." Her giggle was strung too tight.

"You won't be upset?" If this made things weird between us, I'd never forgive myself.

She shook her head. "Don't worry. I'm already over it." Then, seeing me waffling, she grabbed my shoulders and gave me a loving little shove toward Simeon. "Sheyda says yes. She'll do it."

Simeon cocked one eyebrow. "Yes?"

I mustered my courage, then nodded, agreeing to something I'd never in a million years imagined myself doing.

Simeon clapped his hands. "A wallflower turned actress. *Love* it!" He patted my cheek. "Filming starts this Sunday. We'll be doing all of your filming right here at Doughlicious. You'll be marvelous. You'll see."

"Uh-huh," I said weakly, then listened, dazed, as Simeon explained the permission forms my parents would have to sign and the filming schedule. By the time he said good-bye and left the shop, the street outside had grown dark. When I finally became aware of my surroundings again, Mrs. Seng was at the counter, and Kiri was nowhere to be found.

"I better get home," I told Mrs. Seng, then stepped into the kitchen to grab my coat and bag. When I did, I heard muffled sniffles from the bathroom in the back.

"Kiri?" I called through the bathroom door.

"Yeah?" Her voice sounded nasally, like she had a cold. *Was she crying?* My stomach sank.

"Are you okay?"

"'Course I am! I—I'm on Instagram. You know Mom hates that." Her voice rose a notch, reaching toward cheer.

I shifted from one foot to the other, hesitating. "So . . . we're good? 'Cause I'm heading out and I just wanted to make sure—"

"Sheyda! Go! Before Mom catches me slacking!"

"Okay," I said reluctantly. "I'll see you tomorrow morning."

I walked out of the shop and turned toward home. My heart flip-flopped uneasily. What sort of movie mess had I gotten myself into?

Chapter Three

"You? Starring in a movie?" Mina fake-choked on her mouthful of *tahdig*. The crunchy, golden crust from the bottom of the rice pot was Mina's favorite, and I was guessing Mom had served it tonight as a peace offering.

I glanced sheepishly around the dinner table. Mom, Dad, and Mina were all staring openmouthed at me. I knew it was tough to believe, but did *everyone* have to react this way?

"Well." Mom smiled. "That's wonderful news. And I'm glad you're thinking ahead to the cost of drama camp."

Mina choked again. "Wait a sec. You're actually going to let her do this?"

That part was a surprise to me, too. I'd been half hoping that my parents would refuse to sign the permission forms Simeon had given me. Then I'd have an easy out. But here was Mom, giving me an instant blessing.

Dad was nodding, too. "I don't see any reason why Sheyda shouldn't do it." He looked at me. "*Das xoš, aziz.* Well done, darling. It will expand your horizons."

"Yes, and maybe embolden you," Mom seconded.

"Expand her horizons?" Mina dropped her spoon onto her plate with a clatter. "She's going to be around a bunch of celebrities and filmmakers. Aren't you afraid they'll be bad influences on her? Or that she'll fall behind in her schoolwork?"

Mom pressed her fingertips to her temples. "Mina, please don't start—"

"But those were all of the reasons you told me I couldn't go on the ski trip, remember?" Mina glared at me. "And I'm going with my *friends*. I heard Cabe Sadler flirts with every girl on his movie sets. And you're worried about *me*?"

At the mention of Cabe, my stomach flipped. I put down my fork.

"Sheyda's a good student. She uses her time wisely." Dad frowned at Mina. "If your grades weren't teetering in English and geometry, you might have some ground to stand on."

Mina shook her head. "Right. I forgot. My sister. Little Miss Perfect."

I scowled at Mina. "I am not—"

"Nobody's saying that," Mom piped up. "But Sheyda's never broken our rules, or skipped classes—"

"Twice!" Mina jabbed two fingers into the air. "I skipped class twice, and it was because Rehann was having major issues with her parents. I had to help."

"Rehann is exactly why you're not going skiing," Mom said. "She's always in some sort of trouble." Mina rolled her eyes, but what Mom said was true. Last year, Rehann had gotten an in-school suspension for racking up ten unexcused tardies, and she'd spent half of last summer grounded for taking her mom's credit card without permission and going on a serious shopping spree. Rehann's defiance only seemed to make Mina like her more, though.

Dad cleared his throat, maybe as a not-so-subtle signal to Mom. She suddenly seemed to remember that I was still sitting at the table.

Mom gave me a pained smile. "Sheyda shared some good news, and we should celebrate. How about we go out for some gelato after we do the dishes?"

Mina stood up from the table. "I lost my appetite," she said, then disappeared toward our bedroom.

"Me too," I added quietly. "May I be excused?"

Mom and Dad looked at each other. Dad nodded, so I cleared my plate, surreptitiously grabbing a handful of sugary *tuts* from the kitchen. Then I went after Mina. I found her in our room lying across the bottom bunk, earbuds in, thumbs texting speedily on her phone.

"Hey," I tried, but she didn't even raise her head.

We didn't used to be this way. We'd always had very different personalities, but before this year, that hadn't seemed to matter much. Mina was stubborn and outspoken, challenging my parents at every turn, while I was the don't-rock-the-boat people pleaser. Still, Mina had always willingly taken me under her wing, letting me tag along with her and her friends. That had changed last fall when she'd become best friends with Rehann. Everything Rehann did—from the way she dressed to the way she talked—made her seem older. Like, college older. All it took was Rehann to say that having me tag along was like "babysitting," and Mina quit including me. Now when she went shopping in Williamsburg or to the movies in Union Square, I wasn't beside her. I tried to be okay with it. I had Kiri and Doughlicious and my stage designs. But in some ways, it felt like Mina had chosen Rehann's friendship over me, and that stung. More than that, I missed the closeness we'd had.

"I brought you some contraband," I said now, a little louder, then held the handful of pink, sugar-coated *tuts* in front of her face. Her tight scowl loosened as she took one of the almond-and-pistachio candies.

"Thanks," she mumbled, then scooted over a couple inches on the bed, making room for me.

My spirits lifted as I plunked down beside her. "What are you doing?" I popped a *tut* into my mouth, its nutty sweetness coating my tongue.

"Just bemoaning the existence of parents." She gave a stony laugh, then put her phone facedown on the bedspread. She did it quickly, like she didn't want me to catch a glimpse of the screen.

I nudged her with my elbow, grinning. "Were you texting Josh?" I asked teasingly.

In the old days, she would've responded with a grin of her own, but now she snapped, "None of your business!"

I flushed. "Sorry. I didn't mean anything by it—"

Mina shook her head, frowning. "That's just what I need. You saying something in front of Mom and Dad and them getting on my case about being too 'boy crazy.'"

"I—I wouldn't do that," I said haltingly.

Mina blew out a puff of air and slouched against a throw pillow. "Sorry. I know you wouldn't. I'm just so tired of them riding me about everything. And you—" Her phone dinged, and she instantly checked the screen.

"I what?" I pressed. What had she been about to say?

She waved a hand distractedly. "Never mind. That's Rehann. She's outside waiting. We have this school project we're working on at the library tonight . . ." She was off the bed and heading for the door, refusing to meet my eyes. She pressed her lips into a flat line—something she'd done since she was little. I knew what it meant. She was lying.

Where are you really going? I wanted to ask but stopped myself. I only hoped wherever she *was* going with Rehann, she wouldn't get herself into trouble.

"I'll see you later," I called after her. Mina waved and was gone.

I sighed and sat at my desk. I began making a list of supplies I'd buy at Blick art supply store on Bond Street for my set model. More Styrofoam shapes and foam board, balsa wood, some texturing paint. Maybe Mom could take me tomorrow after school. An excited whirring began in my chest. Maybe buying some new supplies would give me the lightning bolt of inspiration I kept searching for.

My excitement, though, was quickly replaced by mild panic as the full realization about the night's events struck me. Mom and Dad had agreed to let me be in the movie! What was I thinking? What were *they* thinking?

I remembered what Mina had said during dinner about Cabe and his flirting. Then, even though I hated myself for it, I grabbed my tablet and yes, I did it. I Googled Cabe Sadler.

No sooner had I hit SEARCH than hundreds of Cabe photos flooded my screen. There he was on the red carpet at last year's Academy Awards. He was smiling suavely in his designer tux, his arm slung casually around the gorgeous tween star Isabel Martinez, who was costarring with him in *Very Valentine*. That was just the beginning. Movie premieres, the Tween Choice Awards, surfing at Zuma Beach . . . there was always a cute girl by his side.

It was ridiculous, really, and maybe even staged. I mean, he was *my* age. But the photos seemed to want to make him look older, as if having his arm around a girl fit his rom-com image. Or maybe that's how *he* wanted the world to see him? Given the conceited way he'd acted around me, so far, that seemed very possible. And very annoying. How was I going to work with him on a movie set?

This was going to be a disaster.

When I rounded the corner onto Third Avenue Sunday morning, my heart jolted into my throat. A half dozen white trailers lined the street, blocking the view of Doughlicious. A group of people looking *way* too sun-kissed to be from the Northeast were unloading expensive-looking cameras and lights from a double-parked truck while others darted around the sidewalk hoisting cords, props, and wardrobe bags. There was an energy to the whole scene that, for a minute, almost made me feel better. Prepping everything for a stage production had always given me a thrill. It was like an unspoken countdown to showtime, when all the work I'd done on a set would finally be displayed. If I'd been one of the crew unloading the truck right now, or setting up props or the set, I would've felt right at home. This time, though, I wasn't going to be behind the scenes.

I gulped. No one had seen me yet. I could backtrack, go home, make up some excuse about being sick—

"Sheyda!" Simeon was hurrying toward me. "To wardrobe and makeup. Pronto." He scooped a hand under my elbow and, before I could protest (or run), he steered me into one of the trailers, then gave a blur of instructions to the two women waiting inside.

"Doughlicious uniform for her, au natural face, but make her eyes pop." He gave me the briefest wave, adding, "See you inside in ten."

"But—" I stammered. *But I don't want to do this!* I tried to scream after him. *I can't do this!*

It was too late. Before I knew it, the two women were pouncing on me with powders, blushes, and eye shadows. They were friendly, introducing themselves as the hair, makeup, and styling team. But there wasn't time to talk, much less time for any modesty. I was out of my own clothes and into a bubblegum-pink dress before I could blink. The women worked quickly and expertly, even as I winced and sneezed when talcum powder filled my nose. They twisted my hair into a French knot and added a vintage flower headband.

"Perfect," one of them said as she pinned a MARIE nametag above the upper left pocket of my dress. "You're good to go."

She opened the trailer door and led me into Doughlicious. I stepped inside and stared. The shop's interior was unrecognizable. Nearly every inch of the walls was covered in vintage donut signs and advertisements. A chandelier made from teacups and silverware hung from the ceiling, and the café tables had been replaced with pink booths.

"They've killed it with tackiness," a voice whispered in my ear, and there was Mrs. Seng, shaking her head forlornly at her shop.

"Oh no." I gave her a reassuring smile. "I like it." Honestly, I did.

"Really?" Mrs. Seng wrinkled her nose. "It looks like a tourist trap now. And we'll have to do business like this until the filming's done."

"I bet it will bring in more customers," I offered optimistically just as I spotted Kiri coming out of the kitchen carrying a beautiful tower of donuts. She wove through the crew members and didn't seem to see me until I reached out, touching her arm.

"Oh, hey!" she said distractedly, then surveyed me up and down. "Wow. Look at you!"

"Is that a bad 'wow' or good 'wow'?" I asked, tugging on my pink dress self-consciously.

"Well, that pink looks great on you, but it reminds me of my costumes from *Grease*."

"Omigod, you're right!" We both giggled, remembering Kiri's poodle skirts.

"I'm kind of glad now that I didn't get the part. I'm so over that Sandra Dee wardrobe." But the way she looked longingly at the camera equipment told me she was still nursing disappointment. "So . . . are you ready for this?"

"I'll never be ready." I blew out a breath.

"You'll do great." She smiled encouragingly.

"Thanks," I said.

A crew member squeezed past with some lighting silks: large, white fabric panels used to soften harsh lighting on set. Then Jillian stepped through the door, looking every bit the director in a cap and a *Donut Go Breaking My Heart* film logo jacket. Cabe was with her, wearing his costume: a pink short-sleeved shirt and khakis. The uniform made his eyes even bluer, his tousled hair even cuter. I blushed, knowing I must look completely ridiculous in my own getup. Then I scolded my cheeks for embarrassing themselves. Didn't they get that he was still a jerk? Apparently not.

"Hey, Cabe!" Kiri began, but Jillian interrupted her.

"Mrs. Seng, Kiri, we're ready to start filming." Jillian motioned to the door. "Please, would you . . .?" It was clear she wanted everyone out of the shop except cast and crew.

I gave Kiri a pleading look, feeling a desperate need for moral support.

"I've got to get these donuts out to the catering table," Kiri said über-cheerily to Cabe. She leaned into me, whispering, "Mom's put me on donut duty all day, so I get to cater to the actors instead of being one. Joy." She rolled her eyes and then added, "You better tell me every single detail later!"

I nodded, feeling equal parts guilty and panicked that she couldn't stay with me. But then she was gone, and Jillian and Simeon were motioning for me and Cabe to join them at the back of the shop. I sucked in a breath and headed straight for certain humiliation.

"Cut!"

I cringed. I was starting to hate that word. I'd heard it at least a dozen times since we started filming what was supposedly a "quick" scene. One thing I'd learned in the last few hours: There was nothing quick about moviemaking. Especially when one of the actresses kept messing up. Namely . . . me!

Jillian sank back in her director's chair, rubbing her forehead and looking like she might cry, scream, or both. Who could blame her? She'd told me the scene was simple.

"So in this scene, it's Prince Dalton's first day working at Doughlicious," she'd explained. "He's in charge of mixing some fresh dough, but he keeps botching it. You—Marie—will walk him through how to do it, but all the while you're wondering why he's acting like he's never seen a kitchen before."

I'd said I'd understood. I'd read through the few lines I had. It *had* seemed simple. Until the cameras started rolling. First, the gaffer, who was in charge of the lighting, couldn't get the shadows to fall in the right places around the kitchen. Then the boom microphone, which was supposed to hover between my head and Cabe's, didn't work and had to be replaced. Finally, after Cabe and I had had our faces re-powdered so many times that I was convinced I looked more clown than person, we tried the scene. That was when things went from bad to worse. I forgot where the on/off switch was on the electric mixer. I spilled a container of sprinkles on the floor. And every time my line came up ("You'd think you'd never held a spatula before in your life"), I froze.

It didn't help that Cabe always seemed to be staring at me. By now he must be fed up with my bloopers. Outside of his scripted lines, he hadn't spoken a word to me, and I felt the tension between us growing.

Now, Jillian and even Simeon were beginning to look like they'd regretted ever giving me the role of Marie in the first place.

"I'm sorry," I said to them. Perspiration beaded my forehead from the heat of the countless lights around the room. "I'm not cut out for this role. Gabe should be working with someone else." A tidal wave of awkward silence crashed over the room, and I wondered what I'd just said that was wrong.

"I think you mean Cabe?" Simeon offered gently.

I slapped my hands to my mouth. "Omigod, yes." I turned to Cabe, who was shaking his head at the floor. "Cabe." Great. Nothing like botching the name of a celebrity to his *face*.

Cabe didn't even acknowledge that I'd spoken. "I'm taking a break," he announced. "It's like a sauna underneath these lights." He nodded toward me. "She'll never get it right if we're melting. Then we'll be here forever."

My cheeks burned. I already knew I was messing up everything. He didn't need to rub it in.

"Apologies, Mr. Sadler." One of the grip assistants hurriedly began rearranging the lights.

"It's not the lights," I said gently to the assistant. "It's me. Sorry."

"Do you always apologize so much?" Cabe asked gruffly.

I hesitated. I'd never thought about it before, but . . . "Maybe," I admitted reluctantly.

"You shouldn't," he said.

"Well, what *should* I do?" I said, feeling a surge of bravery. "Be rude to everyone?" *Like you,* I almost added. Still, he heard the accusation in my tone and met my eyes. I held my breath, preparing to be told off. Then, suddenly, his face softened. I blinked. Huh?

Cabe walked over to Jillian and Simeon. After whispering with them for a few minutes, no doubt about what a *huge* mistake they'd made in hiring me, he grabbed two sodas from a cooler by the back door and held one out to me. I didn't want to accept it from him, but I was parched, so I took it.

I plunked down on the cooler in defeat, and Cabe surprised me by sitting down beside me. "What I meant was, you shouldn't apologize for things that aren't your fault," he said. "Especially when it's me who should be apologizing. The first day I met you, when you gave me that donut bath?"

I opened my mouth to protest, but he held up a hand. "I know! I know!" he said. "It was an accident." He sighed. "You made that clear at the auditions. But the thing is, I've had fans do some really uncool stuff in the past."

I shook my head. "I had no idea who you were, actually."

He laughed. "That's ironic. Around Hollywood, it's pretty impossible for me to go anywhere without people following me with cameras."

I raised an eyebrow. "And . . . you don't like that?" I asked skeptically.

He grimaced. "Hate it. And being in a new place has put me on edge. I don't know New York or what might happen here."

"You're staying in the city until the shooting's finished?" I opened my can of soda and took a sip.

"That's the plan, but depending on what my parents decide, it could end up being longer." Cabe sipped his own soda. "We've been thinking about leaving Hollywood for a while, so they want to scope out some apartments while we're here. I was excited about it at first. But . . ." He shook his head. "I can't get my head around this city. It's another universe."

"You don't like New York?" I asked.

"It's so loud. I hate the cold. And in LA, there's traffic, but not like here. Here it's insane—"

I stifled a laugh. "That's why so many people walk or take the subway . . ."

He stiffened. "Yeah. Walking's not my thing."

I frowned. Of course it wasn't. Why walk when you had a

limo at your beck and call? I felt myself bristling again, annoyed that he was insulting the city I'd been born in and loved.

"Anyway," he added, "I think I gave you the wrong idea about me. So . . . can we start over?"

I blinked, caught off guard. "Okay."

"Good."

"But getting your name wrong isn't exactly getting things off on the right foot, is it?"

He laughed. "Don't worry about that." He leaned closer and whispered, "Between you and me, Cabe's not even my real name."

I stared at him. "What?"

He nodded. "It's true. It's Caleb, but my manager thought 'Cabe' sounded cooler, so . . . here I am. I've gotten used to it, but it'll never be the real deal."

"I like Caleb," I said quietly.

"Thanks." Cabe was silent for a moment. "So why do you?" he asked. "Apologize all the time?"

I shrugged. "I've never noticed that I do." I hesitated,

thinking. "I don't like people being unhappy with me. Or, unhappy with anything, really. I guess I feel like apologizing fixes it."

"I'm not sure it works that way. Sometimes I think people have to fix themselves." Cabe gave me a small smile. I glanced at him quizzically. It almost sounded like he might've been talking about himself. He took a sip of soda and straightened. "So while we have a breather, I was wondering if you could teach me how to mix up some donut batter for real?"

I scoffed. "You don't want to spend your break doing that."

"How else would I spend it?"

I imagined him checking his likes on Instagram or Twitter. Or maybe FaceTiming with his latest celeb crush. "I don't know. I thought you might have to call your manager, or give an inter-view. Or . . ."

"Take a few selfies to send to the tabloids?" He smirked. "That's all famous people do in their free time, right?"

I blushed. "I didn't mean—"

"That's a big assumption, don't you think?"

My blush deepened. He was right. What did I really know about him anyway? "Sorr—" I began, but I stopped myself. "Nope. No more apologies."

Suddenly, the tension on his face evaporated, and we both laughed.

"For the record, I hate selfies. And paparazzi chase *me*, not the other way around." He turned off his cell and set it on the counter to make his point. "I seriously want to learn about donut-making. Research is part of how I get into my roles. Make them believable. What do you say? Please?" He cocked his head to one side in a mischievous puppy-dog sort of way. It was a move I'd seen him use before, in the many Cabe Sadler movies that Kiri had forced me into watching. Girls inevitably swooned when he did it on-screen, but the gesture only raised my suspicions. If he was trying to entrance me into agreeing, it wasn't going to work. I resolved not to let those eyes captivate me. But they were so blue, so striking . . .

"Okay," I said, smiling despite my every attempt not to.

"Great!" We both stood up and Cabe headed for the

enormous floor-to-ceiling mixer. He hefted a ten-pound bag of flour into his arms. "Flour first, right?"

"Wrong," I countered. I pointed to the tall pot that sat on the stove. "We make yeast donuts, so first we have to wake up the yeast. Get it moving so that the dough will rise." I poured a gallon of whole milk into the pot, then pointed to the bag of active dry yeast on an overhead shelf. "We warm the milk, then add the yeast and let the mixture turn frothy."

"Measuring cups?" Cabe asked after we got the bag of yeast open.

I shook my head. "We don't ever use them. When you've done it a thousand times before, you eyeball it. Go ahead, sprinkle some in, until there's a thin layer covering the milk." While Cabe did that, I dropped several hefty pats of butter and sugar into the bottom of the mixer. It was strange, but as we worked, the cameras, lights, and film crew blurred into the background. The more attention I paid to my baking, the less I paid to the chaos all around us.

When the milk started steaming and its surface turned a foamy and light brown, it was ready to go into the mixer. Together, we poured the milk mixture over the butter and sugar.

"Time for the eggs." I set a carton of a dozen in his hands. "Go to town."

He took one egg from the carton. Then, before I could stop him, he dropped the entire egg into the mixer.

"What are you doing?" I cried, peering into the mixer at the smashed egg-and-shell mess. "You're supposed to crack the eggs, not drop them in whole!"

"Oops," Cabe said. "I didn't know. I mean, I don't normally have to cook my own eggs."

I raised an eyebrow. "Come on. It's not like you've never cracked an egg before."

"Um, yeah. It actually is." He shrugged sheepishly. "I never spent much time in the kitchen at home. My schedule never allowed it."

Before I could stop myself, I blurted, "But everyone can crack eggs. I don't care who they are!" His eyes widened in surprise, and there was a hint of hurt behind them. I felt a stab of guilt, scooped out the egg disaster from the mixer, then set another whole egg in his hand.

"Cradle the egg," I said, more gently. I cupped my hand over his, and warm tingles zinged through my fingers. I nearly dropped the egg carton balanced in my other hand. "Um," I stammered, heat flashing over my cheeks, then gave myself a mental shake and refocused. "Okay, so tap it against the side of the mixer. Like this." We tapped the eggshell until it gave way, and I showed him how to pull the shell apart until the yolk slipped into the bowl. He cracked the rest of the eggs perfectly.

I smiled at him. "Good." I turned the mixer on medium speed, letting the ingredients blend into a creamy, pudding-like texture. Cabe lifted the bag of flour, and I nodded. "*Now* the flour. Slow—"

Too late. The flour poured out in an avalanche, and the

moment it hit the mixer's paddle, it shot out in all directions. A blizzard of white spun around us, covering the walls, counters, and floor with flour dust.

"Turn it off! Quick!" Cabe cried as another arc of flour spewed from the mixer. I switched off the mixer, then tried to wipe my eyes clear, coughing and sneezing. I saw a ghostly version of Cabe before me, caked head to toe in white, his blue eyes like the sky breaking through clouds.

I burst out laughing in between sneezes. "You . . . You look ridiculous!"

"Oh yeah?" He grinned. "You should see yourself!" He scooped up a handful of flour and tossed it lightly in my direction. I lobbed some right back at him, and within seconds, the dust was flying all over again. We were breathless with laughter when we heard a half-laughing "Cut!" from across the room.

I froze and blinked as the cameras surrounding us suddenly came into focus again. Jillian was giving us a delighted thumbs-up from her chair.

"That was brilliant! Exactly what we wanted!"

I stared at her as I tried to brush some of the flour from my hair. "But, we weren't on camera. I was just showing Cabe how to make the dough . . ."

"The cameras were rolling the entire time," Jillian said, giving Cabe an approving nod. "Great idea, Cabe."

I turned to him. "What does she mean?"

He gave me an impish smile. "I told them to film us, figuring they could edit later to take what they wanted from the scene."

"You tricked me?" I wanted to be mad, but I felt more relieved than angry. After all, Jillian and the crew were happy, and I'd been spared the nervousness of knowing I was being filmed.

"It wasn't a trick," he said. "I really did want to learn how to make the dough."

"And what about the egg-cracking routine?"

His grin spread wider. "Well, I might have been exaggerating the teensiest bit. I don't do it often, but I *can* crack an egg."

I tossed a dish towel at him. "So you're a better actor than I gave you credit for."

"Okay, kids," Simeon swooped us under his arms and led us out the front door, "that's a wrap for today. Let's get you cleaned up in the trailers."

The brisk air outside was a welcome change from the stuffy heat of the lights indoors, and I breathed in a big sigh of relief. My first day of filming was behind me, and even though it had started off rough, it hadn't ended that badly.

I'd only taken about three steps down the sidewalk before Kiri was running over, talking a mile a minute.

"Omigod, what happened to you?" She gaped. "It was a disaster, wasn't it?" She squeezed my hand. "It's okay. This just isn't your thing . . ."

"Actually," Simeon interrupted, "Sheyda did very well for a rookie. Jillian loved their ad-libbing just now."

"Really?" There was a slight catch in Kiri's tone, as if she didn't quite believe it. "But . . . that's incredible!" She hugged me. "Didn't I say you'd nail it from the very beginning?"

This wasn't exactly true, but this was the Kiri way of offering support, so I nodded my thanks.

"And, Cabe." Kiri swung in Cabe's direction. "I'm sure you were brilliant. You always are."

"Thanks," Cabe said, but a stone curtain fell over his features.

"You know, I'd love to hear about what it's like, the whole celeb lifestyle. How much time do you spend prepping with your scripts? Did you always want to be an actor? Because I feel like it's been my calling since birth—"

Cabe stopped mid-stride. When Kiri looked back confusedly, Cabe tucked his hands into his pockets and mumbled, "I've actually got to get to my trailer. Study up on the script, like you said." He turned abruptly. "See you later." Then he and Simeon were gone.

"Oh! Okay!" Kiri's voice was upbeat as she waved back. "Later!"

"That was rude," I said as soon as Cabe's trailer door shut. "I don't get it. He was fine while we were doing the scene. Nice, even. There were a couple times when I forgot I was talking to someone famous. He sounded sort of . . . normal. And he made the filming fun." I shook my head. "Now he's like a different person."

"He's probably wiped," Kiri said. "Filming is stressful, and then there are his fans." She sighed dreamily. "It's the cost of fame, I guess."

I frowned. I didn't care what the cost of fame was. Cabe didn't have any right to treat Kiri, or anyone else, that way, and the next time I saw him, I was going to tell him so.

Chapter Four

I woke to the incessant buzzing of my alarm and jerked straight up in bed. I glanced at my phone's screen. Oh no. I'd heard Mina getting dressed a while ago, but I'd stayed under the covers. Her high school started an hour before my middle school. I didn't even remember hitting the snooze, but I must have, because now it was almost eight. I had ten minutes to get to school for my meeting with Ms. Feld!

I threw on the first clothes I found, pulled my hair into a mussed knot, then stumbled into the kitchen, grabbing my schoolbag along the way. Mom was standing at the kitchen sink tossing back one last swig of coffee, her keys and purse already in hand. *Great!* I thought. She must've guessed I'd need a ride.

"Mom! Can you drive me to school? I overslept and I'm going to be late for my meeting—"

Her brow knit. "Oh, *aziz*, I'm sorry. I can't today. I just got a call from Mina's guidance counselor, and she wants me to stop by before work." Mom sighed. She was breaking world records in sighing lately. "Something about her attitude in her classes. Apparently several of her teachers are worried about her—oh, what was the word she used?— 'indifference.'" She sighed again. "Thank goodness I've never had to worry about this kind of thing with you."

Right, I thought with an inexplicable twinge of envy, *which is why you never worry about me, period.*

"Maybe I need to spend more time with Mina. This could be a cry for attention?" Mom wondered out loud.

"I don't know, Mom." What I didn't point out was how much of Mom's time Mina already took. Maybe not in face-to-face minutes, but in worry minutes. Mina took hundreds of those from Mom *and* Dad. "Mina's a mystery."

"Okay. I've got to go." Mom planted a quick peck on the top of my head. "If you hurry, you'll only be a few minutes late. Ms. Feld will understand. You're a conscientious student. She knows you'd never be late without reason."

That was true. Being late, missing assignments, slacking in school went against my nature. My teachers said as much in every progress report they'd given me through the years. "Consistently hard-working." "Responsible." "A good role model for others." Those were complimentary words. But part of me worried that they were also boring.

Mom left, and I followed soon after, grabbing a banana and protein bar on my way out. I could only hope I'd make it in time.

Half an hour later, I slumped against my locker, replaying my meeting with Ms. Feld in my head. I'd been a few minutes late, but that hadn't bothered Ms. Feld; my lack of ideas had.

"You still haven't come up with any sketches for your set model?" she'd asked, her voice surprised with a dash of concern. "This doesn't sound like you, Sheyda."

Heat had swept over my face. "I know," I'd admitted. "I just want this model to be perfect. I've had a couple ideas, but none of them have seemed good enough."

She'd pressed her hands into a pyramid, tapping her fingers together. "Good enough for who?"

"The admissions panel. The scholarship committee." I'd shrugged. "Everyone."

She'd leaned forward. "True art isn't about pleasing others. It's about pleasing yourself. Making *your* statement to the world." She'd smiled encouragingly and given me some books on set design. "Look through these and see if anything speaks to you. Inspiration will come."

Now I flipped through the books, eager to spend time with them later. I stuck them into my locker and grabbed my smart tablet for class. As I shut my locker, I heard Kiri's voice, all high notes and giggles. I knew before I looked up that she was in full flirt mode. When I saw her cozied up to Cabe, the two of them walking down the hall together, my stomach somersaulted.

"If you'd started here last fall, you could've had the starring role in our production of *Grease*," Kiri was saying. "You would've been a brilliant Danny Zuko. *So* much better than Liam."

I nearly laughed at that, because back in November, Kiri had thought Liam could do no wrong. Of course, that was before Cabe.

Kiri beamed at him. "We could've played opposite each other."

"Yeah." Cabe flashed a charming smile. "That would've been cool." Then he glanced at his phone and pulled away with a quick, "I've got to get to class. I'll see you after school?"

"It's a date," Kiri singsonged, waving after him.

"A date?" I repeated. She turned to me, her smile huge.

"Not a *date* date, but still. He wants to work on our history project this afternoon in his family's hotel suite."

"But you'll be working at Doughlicious," I began, but when

she clutched my hand and stuck out her lower lip, understanding dawned on me. "*Oh . . .* You want me to cover for you."

"Please? I know you asked Mom if you could have off today, but she'll need at least one of us there."

I hesitated. I'd asked Mrs. Seng if I could have off Monday afternoon to work on my model. If I took Kiri's shift, I'd be putting off the set design for one more day, which I really couldn't afford.

Kiri squeezed my hand. "You'd be doing me such a huge favor. I'd do it for you."

Her puppy-dog eyes were *killing* me. I barely got the "okay" out before she was bouncing on her tiptoes, giving me an excited "Eeeeek!"

"You're incredible!" she gushed. "Do you know his suite has a private pool encased in a heated solarium? He said he was going to give me a whole tour. And if we finish early, his parents might let us use his private screening room. He can stream as many Everest Studio productions as he wants!"

"Sounds cool," I said, my voice straining for enthusiasm I

didn't feel. I kept thinking about that killer smile Cabe had given Kiri. It was the same smile he wore in every poster or red carpet pic I'd seen of him. It was swoon-worthy, all right, but what about genuine?

"Who knows?" Kiri added giddily. "If we hit it off, then I could be his date for the *Very Valentine* movie premiere Valentine's weekend!"

My enthusiasm nosedived into worry. "Isn't that a bit of a stretch? You don't know who he is yet, in real life. And he may even have a Hollywood girlfriend."

Kiri rolled her eyes. "Half of those photos with his costars are staged for the press. I bet his manager concocts those fake, ridiculous romances for his public image." She frowned. "Come on, Sheyda! This is Cabe Sadler!! Asking me to hang out!"

I shook my head. "You're right. You'll have a great time." My dislike of Cabe aside, I had to be happy for Kiri. Right?

"It's almost seven. Just ice one more rack of Bubblegum Drops, and then you can go," Mrs. Seng said.

I dipped another multicolored donut into a bowl of fluorescent-blue icing. Without Kiri, the shop felt strangely empty, despite the lines of customers. Word had gotten around the neighborhood that the shop was being used to shoot a movie, and we were busier today than we'd been in months. I guessed people were stopping by in hopes of catching a glimpse of Cabe or some other celebrity. When they walked into the shop to see everything was business as usual, their expressions betrayed some disappointment. Still, they complimented Mrs. Seng on the shop's new décor and bought extra donuts. Which was why I was icing another three dozen Bubblegum Drops. We'd been so busy that I hadn't even realized how late it was getting until Mrs. Seng pointed it out.

Seven! Once I got home, I still had my homework to do. Would I have any time left over to work on my model? I felt an unfamiliar simmer of irritation with myself. I should've just said no to Kiri. Then I wouldn't feel so stressed about getting everything done.

I quickly finished up the Bubblegum Drops. I'd never

told Mrs. Seng, but the Drops were my least favorite donut. I was more of a purist, and I couldn't understand why anyone would love eating bubblegum-flavor icing. I slid the tray into the display, grabbed my coat and bag, and said good-bye to Mrs. Seng.

When I walked into our apartment, Mom was making chai, tea spiced with cardamom and fennel, in the samovar my grandma brought over from Iran. Our samovar was a beautiful brass, its hand carvings still shining even though the urn, which we used for boiling the tea's water, was decades old. We all took turns polishing it once a month because Mom wouldn't stand for even the slightest hint of tarnish. I drew in a big breath. The smell of Mom's chai was one of my favorite scents in the entire universe, and usually it was one of Mom's favorite ways of unwinding at the end of the workday. Tonight, though, she handed me a cup hurriedly.

"There's a bowl of *ash-e reshteh* for you in the microwave. We haven't eaten yet, but if you're hungry, don't wait." She nodded toward the bedrooms. "Dad and I are talking with Mina about what's happening at school. I thought some chai might help things go more . . . smoothly."

I smiled. "You think chai cures anything, Mom."

"It can't hurt, right?"

I gave Mom an optimistic smile. "Good luck." As soon as she was gone, I heard their voices humming on the other side of Mom and Dad's bedroom door. Maybe Mina would listen, or maybe she'd yell. I sagged against the counter as Mina's voice rose. She was definitely yelling. Suddenly, I felt annoyed. The bad thing about an average New York City apartment was that there weren't a whole lot of places to escape a family feud, unless you wanted to sit on the fire escape. And given the low-teen temps outside, that wasn't an option tonight.

I heated my soup, ate quickly, and went to my room. I started my homework with earbuds in and blaring, drowning out all sounds of arguing. I was so lost in concentration and music that when my cell vibrated at my elbow, I nearly jumped out of my skin. I didn't recognize the number on the caller ID, but I answered anyway.

"Hello?"

"Hello? Sheyda?"

It was Cabe Sadler! I almost fell off my chair.

"It's me," I managed to reply. "Hi?"

"You're wondering why I called," he stated matter-of-factly. The waver of insecurity in his tone surprised me. Then I got it. He was probably used to girls thrilling at the mere sound of his voice. Maybe the fact that I was immune to his charms had him in a tailspin? "I'm supposed to do some read-throughs of the *Donut* script. I thought maybe we could practice our lines together? We'd be better prepared for filming next weekend."

"You mean *I'd* be better prepared," I retorted, then sat back in the chair in disbelief. What had gotten into me? I was never that outspoken.

"That's not what I meant," Cabe said quietly. "Not at all. The truth is that if I can't do a read-through with you, I'll get stuck doing it with my mom." He sighed. "Trust me when I tell you that's all sorts of weird."

I laughed. "I'll give you that. But . . . isn't there somebody else in the cast you'd rather practice with? The actress who's playing Tia?"

"Sonora Grace?" He groaned. "A total diva. She refuses to do any readings. She won't even fly in from Hollywood until the day we start filming her part. She insists that she's too talented to need practice."

"Wow. That's . . . confident of her." Cabe laughed. "But . . . maybe Kiri could help?"

There was a pause and then, "I get it. You don't want to run the lines with me—"

"No!" I blurted. "I just . . . I mean, I thought Kiri was with you? She told me you guys were working on your history project together this afternoon?"

"Oh yeah. We finished a while ago. It didn't take long. She already left." I imagined how disappointed Kiri must've been at having their "date" cut short, but found myself a little relieved, too. "I think Kiri was bummed she couldn't stay," he went on, "but I told her I had too much other work to do."

"Work?" I repeated doubtfully. How much work could a celeb with a private driver have? Then I remembered why he'd called. "Oh. You mean the script reading."

He gave a short laugh. "Acting *is* a legit job, believe it or not."

I blushed. "Of course it is. I didn't mean to sound like it wasn't. But isn't that what film editing is for? In stage acting, if a performer flubs a line, there's no chance for a retake. Everything's in front of a live audience. But with movies, if you make a mistake, it can be edited out."

"That's true, but every mistake costs money and time." His tone became stressed. "Plus, if I'm filming on location somewhere, I've got to keep up with schoolwork or have a tutor on set. At least filming here, I can go to school like everybody else. That's one of the good things about being in this city. That, and garbage shoots."

"Garbage shoots?" I giggled. "That makes absolutely no sense."

"It does when you're the one taking out the trash." He laughed.

"Garbage chutes are so much better than lugging trash cans to the end of a driveway. Trust me."

"Ohhh. *Chutes.*" I laughed. "Let me guess. You have a mile-long driveway back in LA?"

"Not *that* long," he mumbled, "but long enough. And yes, before you make another smart aleck remark, I *do* take out the trash. My parents are on this kick about giving me a normal life. That includes chores."

"What a relief. 'Cause for a minute there I was worried you might be a tiny bit spoiled?" I slapped a hand over my mouth. I couldn't believe I'd done it again—lobbed a jab at Cabe without a second's hesitation.

"Whoa. What happened to the girl who couldn't quit apologizing to everyone yesterday?"

I found myself grinning. "She's still here," I said quietly. Then, in another flash of bravery, I risked, "It's just I haven't made you mad yet. If we talk long enough, I'm sure I'll have something to apologize for. Give it time."

"I'm not so sure about that."

There was a sudden smiling softness to his tone that made my heart drum. "So you like our garbage chutes and our school so far?" I asked to break the silence. "Anything else?"

"Hmmm . . . the skyscrapers are cool, but . . . the throngs of people everywhere and the five million smells coming at you from all directions. That might take a while to get used to."

"The thing about New York City is that once you fall in love with a piece of it, the rest follows. That's how it works its magic. You just need to get to know the city better. That's all."

"I hope you're right," he said. "Because, well, I've been wanting a change. That's part of why we're here."

"What do you mean?"

He sighed. "You don't want to hear about it. You'll think I'm even more spoiled than you already do."

"No . . ." I began to protest, but then Mina came into the room in her pajamas, her hair a newly streaked purple on one side and completely shaved on the other. I gasped. "Your hair," I hissed.

She met my eyes, then shrugged. "What? I was sick of the red." She grinned mischievously.

Oh man. This probably meant Mom and Dad's talk with her hadn't gone over well at all.

"I'm going to bed," Mina announced, stretching catlike onto her duvet, looking pleased with herself, or at least pleased with the shock she'd give Mom and Dad in the morning. "Can you take your confab with Kiri into another room so you don't keep me awake?"

A slow simmer began in my stomach. Mina saying she was going to bed translated into Mina lying in the dark and Snapchatting with Rehann and Josh. What difference did it make whether I stayed in the room or not? Besides, it was my room, too. I wanted to say something. I *should* say something. But if I protested now it would only start a fight with her.

"Sounds like you need to go?" Cabe said.

"Um . . ." My mind whirled as I realized two things: 1. We'd never gotten around to reading the script. 2. I didn't want to hang up.

"We can do the read-through another time," he went on, and then added, more quietly, "It's almost nine anyway, and I don't want you to get in trouble."

We'd been on the phone for half an hour, but it had only seemed like a few minutes. How had time flown so quickly?

"Sheyda?" Cabe's voice interrupted my thoughts. "Are you still there?"

"Sorry! Yes, I'm here!" I blurted.

"You said the *s* word." Cabe gave a short laugh.

"I know. Because I *am* sorry, but I do have to go." Mina was waiting, tapping her foot impatiently. "I'll see you at school tomorrow."

"Sounds good." I detected the slightest shift in his tone, back to something more impersonal. Maybe it wasn't often that he had people opting out of conversations with him. Or maybe he was annoyed that we hadn't gotten around to the script. I didn't know, but I had a sinking feeling that I'd read our phone chat all wrong. The laughs were just part of the fame act Cabe had to put on, making nice with everyone so he wouldn't get any bad press.

I said good-bye and ended the call. A second later, my cell vibrated with a text from Kiri:

CAN'T STOP ☺! DEVELOPING A SERIOUS CABE CRUSH! TEXT BACK ASAP! DONUTS!

She'd used our code word: donuts. When one of us used it, the other one had to drop everything to talk. It was supposed to be for emergencies only (like the sobbing, you-had-a-huge-fight-with-your-parents-and-they-grounded-you-for-life type of emergencies), but Kiri used it for pretty much everything. She'd keep texting if I didn't respond. Normally, I didn't mind. But tonight, I couldn't deal.

Another day had come and gone without me working on my model, and I'd just had a completely confusing conversation with a boy whose face could launch a thousand likes on Instagram.

My heart pounded as I turned off my cell, slipped on my pajamas, and crawled into bed. For once, I didn't feel like being anyone's cheerleader or sounding board. Not tonight. Not when I couldn't even make sense of myself.

Chapter Five

"Where *were* you last night?" Those were the first words Kiri said to me the next morning when I picked her up on my way to school. She handed me two of the four pastry boxes of Doughlicious donuts cradled in her arms. Every Tuesday we brought donuts to school for the staff lounge room. Principal Gomez, a devout donut lover, had a standing account with Mrs. Seng. I tucked the still-warm boxes under my arm, breathing in their sugary aroma.

"I was home," I said cryptically. "I was wiped so I went to bed early." I pulled a slip of paper out of my pocket and handed it to her. "Here's a new donut recipe for your mom. I saw it on Pinterest this morning and tweaked it a little. Orange Candy Crush. Maybe we can try it at the shop."

Kiri shot me a doubtful look. "You had time to find my mom another recipe, but you didn't text *me* back!"

"Finding a new recipe takes two seconds," I said. "I was just trying to help your mom out."

"Mom is donut-crazy enough without your help. Besides, I needed to talk to you."

"Sorry," I said, then cringed. "We can talk now."

"Now?" She harrumphed, then laid the back of her hand against her forehead like she was some tragic heroine. "*Now* my moment of dire need has passed."

"Nice theatrics, but you're not dying." I laughed, nudging her with my elbow. "And I bet if you try *really* hard, your moment will come back to you." We paused to cross St. Mark's Place for the walk north to Ninth Street. Some people hurried past on their way to work, while others strolled with dogs or coffee at a leisurely pace. Rectangles of sky bordered the roofs of the brown-stones and taller apartment buildings, making me feel like I was under a patchwork quilt. I loved that view, and the bright sky made me think of Cabe's eyes. My heart flipped, but I ignored it. "Anyway," I went on, "Mina and my parents are doing battle over her attitude, and Mina shaved half her head last night, so it wasn't the best time for chats."

"Wow. She's more wild-child every day. It's impressive."

"Yeah, except you don't have to live with it. This morning, she told my parents she'd rather lick subway handrails than partici-pate in class."

Kiri gagged, sidestepping a frozen puddle of spilled coffee on the sidewalk. "Omigod, does she have any idea how many germs are on those things?"

I laughed. "Yeah, well, we'll see who caves first." I thought about the tension oozing like toxic mud through our house right now. Mom was coming home early today to spend some "quality time" with Mina. Mom had said, "Oh, of course I want to spend time with you, too, Sheyda. Only I thought you might be busy with your set design." It came across as more afterthought than invite, making me feel oddly left out. So, maybe I'd stop by the shop with Kiri after school instead. It would be better than going home to more Mina drama. What would she do next? Pierce her belly button?

"So," I said to Kiri now, wanting to distract myself, "are you going to spill how it went with Cabe?"

"I'm not sure if you deserve it after dissing me last night." She mock glared, then broke into a smile. "O–kaaay. Cabe is ador-able, *and* he's smart. He had this idea about doing our history project on Charlie Chaplin. He's going to dress up as Chaplin for our presentation, and I'll be the actress Mary Pickford, and we're going to act out a silent film in class! Isn't that brilliant?"

I nodded, smiling.

"I'm so lucky to have him as my partner, and, Sheyda . . ." She squeezed my hand. "I really think he might ask me to go to the *Very Valentine* premiere with him!"

I slowed my pace. "What makes you think that?"

"He mentioned the premiere a bunch of times, almost like he

was dropping hints about it. *And* he said his manager's pushing him to find a date ASAP."

"Did he say he wanted to go with *you*?"

Her smile drooped at the corners. "Well . . . no. Not yet. He's probably working up to it." Her eyebrows crinkled in frustration. "Sheyda! You're giving me your don't-get-carried-away look."

"I am?" I shrugged sheepishly. "For all we know, Cabe already has lines of girls waiting to go with him, and—"

"What? You don't think I'd live up to his Hollywood standards?" She pushed her mittened hands into her coat pockets, a gesture that made her look amusingly like a little girl getting ready to tantrum.

"That's not what I'm saying at all." We stopped in front of the school steps. "I'm just worried you might get hurt, that's all."

Kiri waved a dismissing hand. "I can hold my own, and even if it doesn't turn into anything, I'm fine with that. I don't have to really, *really* like him. Just one photo of me on his arm could launch my career . . ."

"Wait a sec." I frowned. I didn't like what I was hearing. "What do you mean?"

She shrugged. "Nothing! Only that hanging out with him might be a good chance for me to make some studio connections." She giggled awkwardly, not wanting to meet my eyes. I knew how much Kiri wanted a shot at film acting, but this sounded dangerously like she wanted to use Cabe as a means to that end. She could be impulsive like that, carried away by some far-fetched idea. Last year she'd posted videos on YouTube of herself acting out lines from famous movies, in hopes of being "discovered." The first few had been fun, but then it turned into a video every day, and finally Mrs. Seng had to confiscate Kiri's cell for a month to put an end to it. Kiri glanced at me and saw exactly what I was thinking.

"Don't look at me like that!" she exclaimed. "I'm not going to get carried away! But my soul will shrivel into a raisin if I have to bake donuts the rest of my life. My spirit won't be reined in by dough! It needs excitement, and sunshine, and—" She clutched her hands to her chest. "A star on the Hollywood Walk of Fame."

I burst out laughing, and she slapped my arm. "I'm just going to see where this takes me, that's all. And of course it'll be fun getting to know Cabe better, too." She suddenly craned her neck around me and waved. "Cabe!"

I turned to see Cabe emerging from his limo. Kiri skipped down the sidewalk toward him in her peep-toe booties and pleated skirt. She tucked her arm through his with a confidence that said they were already a couple. Cabe, for his part, offered up a smile, but then stepped out just enough to put a small space between them.

"I was just telling Sheyda about your genius idea for our project!" Kiri said.

"Hi." Cabe glanced at me, still smiling, and his tan cheeks turned a dark shade of peach. I did a double take. It could've been the crisp air, or . . . He couldn't possibly be blushing! Could he? "I'm no genius. It was a choice between impersonating Charlie Chaplin or doing a paper about him, and my writing's pretty pathetic."

"I'm sure you're great at everything you do," Kiri said.

Cabe shook his head. "Nobody's like that," he said directly.

"Well, I'm so glad we're partners," Kiri continued, "because I'd be at a total loss for ideas if it weren't for you."

Cabe shifted, stamping his boots on the sidewalk as the wind picked up. One by one, other students were starting to form a huddle around us, like Cabe had some sort of magical, gravitational pull. The more crowded the sidewalk became, the farther Cabe's head drew into his upturned coat collar. "It's freezing out here and I have to get to homeroom to finish up a math worksheet," he said abruptly. "See you in history," he added to Kiri, and just like that, he was taking the steps two at a time and disappearing through the school doors.

There was a wilting inside me. It wasn't as if I'd been expecting him to pay more attention to me after our phone call last night. Aside from his quick hi just now, though, he'd left without even giving me a second glance.

Kiri and I went inside and dropped off the donuts in the

lounge room, then headed to our first period classes. Through it all, one question stayed in my mind: Were Cabe and I friends or weren't we? I didn't have a clue.

"Remember the raisin?" Kiri said when we met at my locker after the final bell. She pretended to pound her head against the locker next to mine. "The soul shriveling? It's happening."

I surveyed her face. "It can't be. I see no shriveling."

She held up her cell phone. "Mom texted me. Donut Planet debuted a new donut today. The Caramel Colossal. Apparently it's so amazing it's trending on Instagram, Twitter, and Snapchat. She wants me to walk downtown to try one." She tensed her face in a dead-on impression of her mom. "'Kiri, competition is our best teacher,'" she mimicked, crossing her arms. "Ugh. Mom doesn't ever get it. I can't tell the difference between our donuts and theirs. They taste the same to me—too sweet, too sticky. What I really want to do is stream the Golden Globes with Val. She asked me over. I didn't get to watch them Sunday because of all the craziness with the filming at the shop. I haven't even seen half the dresses yet. So I thought if you didn't already have plans that you might want to . . ."

"Go to Donut Planet instead?" I offered. It would be perfect—I could stay out of Mina's and Mom's hair (or, in Mina's case, lack thereof), and then maybe I could go to the library afterward to work on my model. I didn't mind taste testing donuts. It was one of my favorite parts of helping out at Doughlicious. "Sure, I'll go."

Kiri's face brightened. "Really?" I nodded and she grabbed me in a thank-you hug, then pulled away, looking guilty. "Val told me to ask you over, too. Even Phoebe's coming."

"Phoebe?" I repeated. That was a surprise. She'd never been into Hollywood glam.

Kiri nodded. "There's a foreign film she loves that's up for a visual effects award. But I figured . . . well, the Golden Globes aren't really your thing."

I knew that. I also knew that Kiri would share her hundred posts of the red-carpet gowns with me on Pinterest later, so I wouldn't really be missing out on much. Still, I wondered if Kiri had waited until after I'd committed to tell me about Val and Phoebe, so it would be harder for me to change my mind. What did it matter though? She was my best friend, and I wanted to do this for her. I didn't care about the Golden Globes anyway. "You're right," I affirmed. "Totally not my thing." I pulled out my phone. "I'll let my mom know."

Just then, Val and Phoebe waved from down the hallway and Kiri stepped toward them, blowing me exuberant kisses. "You're a goddess! Love you!"

"We'll miss you, Sheyda!" Val called out while Phoebe rolled her eyes drolly, warning Val and Kiri, "I'm only coming for the popcorn. Don't expect me to gush over dresses and shoes."

After they left, I texted Mom and then gathered my home-work and books together. I frowned when Mom texted back: OK TO DONUT PLANET. HAVE U HEARD FROM MINA? SHE'S NOT HOME. MUST HAVE FORGOTTEN I WAS COMING HOME EARLY? ☹

I sighed. Forgotten, or more likely, ditched Mom in favor of hang-time with Rehann and Josh. I sent a quick NO WORD

FROM MINA to Mom, then headed for the doors. For a second, I thought about going home to cheer up Mom.

Then I spotted Cabe standing inside the doors, peering through the window and frowning. If I didn't know better, I would've guessed he was trying to hide from something, or someone.

"If you're waiting for the weather to warm up," I said, "you'll be standing here until April."

He started at the sound of my voice, but his expression instantly recovered, smoothing into relief. "I'm so glad it's you!"

Warmth washed over me. He was? "Are you okay?" I asked. "You don't look so great." Omigod. Had I just told the face that graced every teen magazine on the planet that it looked *bad*?

Cabe snorted. "Are you always so blunt?"

"Never." I shook my head adamantly. "Only with you, for some bizarre reason."

He laughed once, a single sad note. "I've got a problem. Ben, my driver, was supposed to be waiting for me, but he called to say he's stuck in traffic uptown." He sighed. "It sounds lame to be complaining about this, but . . . well, look."

I peeked through the window and saw a mob scene. There were some lingering kids from our school, but also dozens of paparazzi, their cameras poised for photo ops.

"Yeesh. They're persistent, aren't they?"

"Never ending." The blue tides of his eyes darkened into a stormy cobalt. "Normally Principal Gomez lets me leave school a few minutes early to sneak out, but he's out sick today, and the assistant principal must've forgotten. If I go out there, they'll follow me for hours. Just for once, I'd love to be ignored."

Poor guy, he looked desperate. I touched his arm. "Come on. I know another way out."

He nodded gratefully and followed me without any questions. There was an emergency exit at the back of the theater stage that led into the alley behind the school building.

"If we go down this alley," I explained as we skirted the school's Dumpsters, "it'll spit us out on Tenth Street. We can walk over to Avenue A from there."

"Is that on your way home?" he asked. "I don't want to be a pain."

"You're not," I said, surprised by his thoughtfulness. "Anyway, I need to stop at another donut place to do some taste testing."

"Hey!" He smiled. "Would you mind if I tagged along? It might be cool to try out some other donut shops while I'm in town. It would help me get more into my Dalton character. Besides, I haven't seen much of the city yet. Since you love it so much, you're the perfect person to show me around."

Nervousness made my pulse spring. It was one thing talking to Cabe in my comfort zone at home. It was another being face-to-face with him. This was more of a Kiri-style idea, or maybe even a Mina one. It felt impulsive—fun but unnerving. But maybe that was just it. I'd been worried about being boring. Maybe I needed more surprises and less overthinking. I took a deep breath. "Sure you can come along! But . . . we'll be on foot," I warned teasingly. "You'll have to actually walk."

"Funny." He rolled his eyes, but he was still smiling. "It's not actual walking I don't like. It's not being left alone while I'm walking."

"Oh, that makes sense."

Since the paparazzi were waiting at the school entrance, we'd managed to avoid them. Even when he saw that the sidewalk was clear of reporters, though, Cabe was wary. He slipped on sunglasses and a wool hat. "I'm not sure this is going to be enough. Someone's going to recognize me."

"I doubt it," I said half jokingly, but when he didn't even crack a smile, I realized how much he dreaded the prospect. Then, an idea struck, and I picked up the pace. "I think I have a solution."

He looked at me questioningly. We turned onto St. Mark's Place and came to a shop front piled high with teetering hats— boleros, sombreros, newsboys, berets. Next door was Wonky Wigs & More, across the street was a vintage clothing store, and above that was a flashing sign advertising psychic readings. "This is one of my favorite streets in Manhattan. You're Cabe Sadler now, but pop into a couple of these shops and you'll walk out as an entirely different person."

He moved down the sidewalk, eyeing the bizarre mishmash of merchandise. He stopped in front of a red curly wig, complete with detachable fake beard. He picked it up, then grabbed a sleek fluorescent-purple wig and handed it to me. "I'm only game if you are."

I giggled, my heart racing. Here it was again. A choice between boring, play-by-the-rules Sheyda and someone new, someone unpredictable. I slipped the wig on over my hair, and, barely believing what I was doing, said, "I'm in."

Fifteen minutes later, we'd dipped into and out of nearly every store on the block. As we shopped, I'd told Cabe what I knew about the history of St. Mark's Place, how it had been a street full of boarding houses for immigrants at one point in history, had become an underground hippie hangout in the '60s, and now was a huge draw for tourists visiting the city.

"You can buy an egg cream two doors down from a falafel," I said. "You can find a million different smells, colors, and tastes all within five feet of each other." I smiled. "How many places on the planet can you say that about?"

"True," Cabe said, pulling an orange-and-green pom-pommed poncho from a clothing rack and slipping it over his coat. I laughed when he tossed me a lime-green pleather blazer. I slid it over my sweater, then struck a ridiculous pose, and we both cracked up.

"That's one of the things I love the most about SoCal," Cabe said as we walked to the counter to pay. "The smell of the Pacific Ocean. If we end up staying here, I'll really miss that."

The salesclerk asked if we wanted shopping bags, but we glanced at each other and shook our heads, slipping on our disguises.

We stepped outside and into the flow of people strolling by. "I guess every home feels that way," I said. "Like a place you leave a little bit of love behind in. My mom told me my grandma used to talk about her village in Iran like there was still a small part of her there, selling fresh baklava at market, laughing with her friends. Cabe smiled. "What I mean is, just like you leave a little love behind in places you've lived, I think you bring a little of every home with you, wherever you go, too."

"I've never thought of it like that before." His eyes settled on mine and lingered thoughtfully. "I like the idea that places shape you in a forever kind of way. Like people, and experiences, too." He stopped so suddenly mid-step that I collided into his side. His hand caught my waist to steady me, and a flurry of butterflies took flight inside me.

"Check out that poster." His eyes fixed on a Walkerspace Theater ad for an upcoming play. "It says it's a debut from a new playwright. That sounds cool."

I nodded. "It's Off Broadway. The East Village and SoHo have a lot of smaller theaters. My parents have taken me to a bunch of them. You get to see some great original performances and sometimes actors and actresses before they become famous."

He looked at the poster for a long minute. "That's how I started," he said quietly. "Onstage, in front of a live audience. My parents say I was acting out scenes from books and movies even as a toddler. So I auditioned for the role of Tiny Tim in our community theater's *A Christmas Carol*." He looked lost in the happy memory. "This was back when we lived in Ventura

County, north of LA. Anyway, an uncle of one of the cast members came on opening night. He turned out to be a movie producer. He talked with my parents after the show, and before I knew it, I had a small role in a movie. Then more roles came, we moved to LA, and—"

"The rest is cinematic history?" I finished for him.

"Yup." He laughed softly, but also, I thought, sadly. "Nothing since *A Christmas Carol* has ever felt as real, somehow, not even life. Hollywood is so groomed, so contrived, and with all the special effects, movies are more like that, too. Onstage, you feel the crowd, watching, waiting, reacting. Every performance and every audience is a little different. Something fresh."

"You miss it." I could hear it in his tone.

He nodded. "Because cameras? They only record. They don't respond. They don't really *see* you, get what you're trying to do."

"That's why I love set design, too," I said. "It's tangible. I can see the end product, but I also build it. You know that day you saw me on the catwalk at the school theater?" He nodded. "It's actually a sort of . . . special place for me. I sit up there sometimes, for perspective. From up there, I have a better idea of how space is used onstage. Like how parts of the set fit together. A lot of set design involves creating illusions of depth or texture on flat surfaces."

"Sounds cool," he said. "Like the way old movie sets were made with scenic backdrops and stuff, when scenes were all shot indoors instead of on location."

We stood together, looking at the poster in comfortable silence until he straightened and said, "So. Donuts?"

There was so much more I wanted to ask him about—well, everything. I nodded and smiled. "Absolutely."

We walked the rest of the way to Essex Street laughing at our ridiculous outfits, then laughing even more that no one so much as gave us a second glance. It was a warm enough day that I could get away with wearing the blazer without my coat, and even though Cabe joked that my clothes were blinding him, they felt strangely freeing. The longer I kept my purple wig on, the braver I felt. It made me more talkative and more relaxed. By the time we stepped through the door of Donut Planet, I realized with pleasant surprise that we'd just walked the last ten blocks talking nonstop. We ordered an array of donuts and tucked into a booth to try them one by one.

Cabe tried the Caramel Colossal first. When he cut into it with a plastic knife, a river of gooey caramel poured out of its center. "Whoa. That's a lot of caramel." He popped a piece into his mouth, chewed, and thought. "A delectable palette of rich toffee flavors," he said in a British accent, "with buttery undertones."

I giggled, then took a bite myself. "Not bad," I admitted, "but it would be better topped with honey-roasted pecans."

"Totally," he agreed. "Which one next?"

I held up the Banana Cream Pie. "This one is *sooo* good. We need to try something like this at Doughlicious. But maybe with some pineapple, too."

"And coconut shavings," he added. I texted myself a note about it. We tried the Mango Cobbler next, and then the Tiramisu bear claw. "So," I said between bites, "you haven't told me yet why your family's thinking about moving here."

"Actually . . . it's for me. For a change. There's so much

pressure in Hollywood to have a certain lifestyle. A lot of kids our age have a tough time with it. I landed my first major role in a movie when I was six." He hesitated, as if he expected me to blurt out the name of the movie instantly. When I didn't, he said, "*Kindergarten Spy*? It was a huge blockbuster."

I shrugged sheepishly. "I haven't heard of it."

He stared at me, then laughed. "That's so great. I mean, I've never met anyone my age who *didn't* see that movie. It's nice to finally know someone who doesn't have this image of me as a thumb-sucking spy in an Inspector Gadget overcoat."

I smiled. "You sucked your thumb?"

"For the *part*," he mumbled.

I giggled, but when he glared, I held up my hands. "I'm not judging. I slept with a stuffed duck named Tibs until I was ten. I still have him." Then I added, "Besides, I prefer imagining you as Tiny Tim anyway."

He smiled. "Thanks. Anyway, my parents are really rooting for me to like it here. I'm not sure yet, but I don't want to disappoint them."

"I worry about that, too," I said quietly. "Not just with my parents. With everyone. I just hate the thought that I'd ever accidentally hurt somebody's feelings."

He studied my face. "So you overcompensate by never saying anything to rock the boat?"

I shrugged. "Maybe. I don't know. I'm still not even sure why I agreed to be Marie in your movie," I admitted. "That's not who I am."

His gaze turned intense, and he leaned toward me like I was the only person in the entire room who mattered. "So, who are you then?"

I hesitated, a self-protective instinct kicking in. What if that was just a line he used with every girl? I didn't want to fall for some insincere flirtation trick.

"You don't want to know," I said, focusing on twisting the napkin in my hands into a tight paper rope.

He sat back, frustration streaking across his face. "You're good at deflecting, but I'm not giving up."

There was an honesty to his tone that broke through my

doubt. In that moment, I believed him. I smiled hesitantly. "Okay. Here goes." I took a deep breath. "I think a lot of things I don't say. I sit in the back row in class so I'm not called on. I hide in plain sight so much that even my own family forgets about me sometimes."

"Really?"

I nodded, and suddenly, it was like the floodgates had opened. I wasn't just offering up a vague description of myself; I was pouring out details. About my set design idea drought. About Mina, and how we used to be close but now she hardly spoke to me, and about how my parents seemed to spend all their time lately worrying about her.

"It's not that I don't love her, because of course I do," I said. "But I've got stuff going on, too, and Mom and Dad are oblivious. Like, I've been trying to figure out my set design for weeks, and I'm stuck. *Really* stuck. And they don't have a clue. Not that they could help anyway, but it would just be nice to have them ask me."

He nodded. "I hear that. Have you told them that, though?"

"No!" I blurted. "They're way too stressed about Mina." I focused my attention on the remaining donuts and bit into a Merry Mermaid donut—an odd combination of candy seashells, coconut, blue icing, and sea salt. "Ugh. Definitely not a fan." I grimaced and Cabe laughed.

"You're afraid to tell them," he said, and I couldn't deny it. "But they'll still love you. That kind of love is *real*." He studied the donut crumbs on his plate. "People think that when you're famous, you're surrounded by people who love you. But fans love the *idea* of you, not who you really are. So that makes it weirdly lonely. I'm so glad my parents are around, and real, you know? Real is so much better than going incognito." He stuck a hand under his wig and fake beard, scratching. "Speaking of incognito, this thing is itching like crazy." With that, he yanked the whole disguise off his face, then sighed in relief. "So much better."

There was a second when we both glanced around, half expecting a horde of fans to come screaming. The shop was crowded with customers, but no one glanced our way.

"See?" I said. "This is a huge plus for Manhattan. New Yorkers may know who you are, but they don't care. We're way too cool to chase celebs. This town is all about anonymity."

Cabe burst out laughing. "You're giving me a hard sell!"

"Me? Never!"

"Or . . . maybe you just want me to stay?"

I blushed as his words hung in the air, then I cleared my throat, changing the topic. "Would you still be able to act if you moved here?"

"Oh, sure," Cabe said. "I'd have to travel to LA quite a bit, but I could never quit acting. I love it too much. Mom and Dad were older when they had me, and the money I make with movies has helped them retire. But, I've thought about cutting back on movie roles for a while, to try doing . . ." He paused. "What *would* I do?"

I tossed a napkin at him. "Seriously? Go to school. Do homework. Play sports. Do stuff other kids do."

"Well, I surf."

"If you surfed in the East River, you might grow an extra limb," I joked.

He smiled. "Living like a non-celeb, huh? I want it, but it would also be bizarre for a while, like breathing underwater."

"Totally. As bizarre as taking out the trash," I deadpanned, then ducked as a napkin flew my direction. We both grinned.

"Well, it's not happening right now, so I shouldn't overthink it. You, on the other hand, have your deadline coming up and no set-design idea. *That* is a right-now problem."

"Yeah, I'd take a lightbulb moment for sure. But . . . *Romeo and Juliet*? It's been done so many times. I get stuck in a loop where all I can think about is those versions and nothing new."

"Too bad you can't go back in time to see it performed for the first time in the Globe Theatre in London," Cabe said. "That would have been incredible *and* inspiring."

We sat in silence for a few minutes, lost in thought. Then it happened. My eureka moment. "That's it!" I cried. "That's the fresh spin." Cabe stared at me, waiting. I slapped a hand down on the table. "Time travel!" My pulse quickened. "I could give Romeo and Juliet an actual future, instead of tragedy. They discover a loop in time and they escape into it, while everyone else believes they're dead."

Cabe smiled. "Whoa. Now *that's* different."

"And the set could have a past and future," I rambled on, getting excited. "I could exaggerate the technology of the future, really play up the strangeness of the architecture." My mind flooded with images, and I whipped out my phone to text myself notes. I got so caught up that I forgot Cabe was there, until he said a soft "Hey."

I glanced up. "Omigod. I finally have a picture of what I want to do." I beamed. "It's like—"

"A lightbulb?" he finished for me.

"More like a thousand." I sat back in the booth. "What a relief." I took a big bite of the last donut, a Licorice Delight, topped with licorice bits with a huckleberry and meringue center. "Mmmm, this one is amazing. Or maybe it just tastes better because I *feel* so much better . . ." I stopped when I noticed Cabe looking at me with twinkling eyes, his lips tight from holding in laughter.

"What?" I asked blankly.

He lifted his hand to my face. "You've got some meringue . . ." His thumb gently brushed the corner of my mouth. I caught my breath, and at that second, I heard the telltale click of a camera. A flash exploded in our faces. Cabe and I whipped around to see a stranger grinning as her camera's shutter fired rapidly.

"Oh no," Cabe mumbled, leaping out of the booth and grabbing my hand. "Let's get out of here."

We ran out of the shop and down the block, the woman following on our heels.

"Cabe, wait! I'm with the *Post*. Just a couple of questions about your new friend . . ." Her voice faded into the city's din.

"I don't know where I'm going!" Cabe said as we breezed through an intersection just before the traffic light changed. I checked the cross streets, a mental map of the city popping into my head.

"Follow me," I said, then pulled ahead of him. We made a quick turn onto Mulberry Street and into Little Italy. Tourists spilled in and out of restaurants under the strings of lights crisscrossing the narrow street. I wove through the throngs with Cabe beside me, ducking between people in hopes of losing the reporter. Within minutes, we'd navigated onto Bowery and ended up at the entrance to Albert's Garden.

I looked over my shoulder, but the reporter was long gone. "Come on." I motioned Cabe to follow me inside the garden gates. "It's not always open to the public, but this is one of my favorite neighborhood haunts. I wish you could see it in the springtime. It's so beautiful." Even in the depths of winter, though, the bare trees and snow-covered garden patches had a stark loveliness.

We sat down on one of the scrolled iron benches, and Cabe texted his driver. "Ben can pick us up from here and take you home first. Then I should get back to the hotel before any more press hounds track me down." There was a strain on his face that hadn't been there at Doughnut Plant, and I found myself wishing our afternoon hadn't been spoiled by paparazzi. "It is nice here," he added, taking in the garden.

We passed a few minutes in contented silence, and I was

disappointed when Ben arrived to drive us home. I'd never ridden in a limo before, but I was too distracted by my swirling thoughts to enjoy the luxurious ride.

When I stepped out onto the curb in front of my apartment building, I gave Cabe a smile. "Thanks for coming with me," I said. "And for helping me with an idea for my model."

He smiled back. "I can't take credit for that. I might've helped with the spark, but it was *your* lightbulb. And thanks for letting me tag along. It was fun, getting to see the city through your eyes."

"Did I change your mind about it?"

"Too soon to tell." His gaze held mine. "But I liked you trying."

Then the car door shut, and the limo drove off. It had been a great afternoon. Maybe too great. Being friends with a megastar was one thing, but what about this new, persistent fluttering in my heart? It made me nervous. Which was why I almost jumped out of my skin when my cell rang inside my coat pocket.

"Okay, spill it." Kiri's voice was tight and tense. "What's going on between you and Cabe?"

"What?" It was like she could see inside my brain. "Nothing. I mean . . . what are you talking about?"

She heaved a breath. "I'm talking about the photo of the two of you at Doughnut Plant." There was silence while she waited for this to sink in. "It's gone viral. Instagram, Snapchat. Everywhere. Don't tell me you haven't seen it?"

"Um . . ." Oh no. She couldn't be talking about the pic snapped by the reporter. My phone dinged again with an Instagram share message from Kiri. I held my breath and stared at the photo. There it was. Cabe wiping the icing from my mouth as I smiled at him with this smitten expression. A caption blazed under the photo: CABE WITH MYSTERY GIRL. I closed my eyes and sank onto our front stoop. "Kiri, this is a mistake. Some reporter took the picture. I had icing on my face. Cabe pointed it out. That was it."

"Are you sure?" Kiri's tone was worried, but also tinged with—what? Anger? Jealousy? I didn't want to think about it. I only wanted to make it go away. "Look, Sheyda, it's no secret that Cabe's easy to fall for. I'm sure you didn't mean for this to happen—"

"Wait. Kiri. Nothing's happened." I gripped the phone. "I swear!"

There was silence, and then a long relieved sigh. "Oh, Sheyda. I'm so glad. I mean, you'd never be comfortable in the spotlight with him."

"I might be." My whole body tensed. Suddenly, I didn't feel like reassuring Kiri anymore. But why? Why was I getting so defensive when what she was saying was spot-on?

"Never mind about that. It doesn't matter. I'm sorry I freaked. If something was going on with you and Cabe, I know you'd be honest with me. Because I've worshipped him since forever, and it wouldn't be fair for . . . for . . ."

"For what? For me to have him instead of you?" My voice sounded harder than I'd meant it to. But I realized I didn't want to be fighting with Kiri over this. Not when there wasn't anything real to fight about. "I didn't mean that," I added hurriedly.

"I just meant . . . we were only hanging out as friends." It was the truth, but something about saying it felt insincere.

After another long pause, Kiri said, "Okay." Her voice was back to normal again, and relief washed over me, along with a serious reality check. How had I even been contemplating a flutter over Cabe? It was wrong, not just because he'd never fall for someone like me, but because Kiri liked him. I couldn't mess with that.

"Are we okay?" I asked.

"Of course we are." Her voice was bright, but there was a new reserve in it that gave me a twinge of sadness, like we'd somehow drifted apart in the span of a few short minutes. "I believe you, but I don't know how you're going to convince everyone else. Now the photo's out there for the whole world to see."

"Everything will be fine." I strained for a certainty I didn't feel. "How much of a problem can one photo cause?"

Chapter Six

"Sheyda." Someone was shaking my shoulder gently, then not so gently. "Sheyda! Wake up!"

I opened my eyes to find Mina's face inches from my own. I was groggy, having stayed up late working on my model. Now that I had a solid idea of what I wanted to do, sketches had poured out of me. I'd be ready to start cutting pieces for stairs and backdrops as soon as I finished up filming at Doughlicious tonight.

"Mina," I groaned. "What?"

"You should think about wearing your hair up today and borrowing some of my makeup." She shook her head in amazement. "At least Mom and Dad can't blame me for this one."

I pulled a pillow over my head. "I don't know what you're talking about."

"I'm talking about this." She yanked me out of bed and pulled me to the window.

I squinted into the brightness streaming through the blinds, then gripped the windowsill. "Oh no." On the sidewalk in front of our building huddled a crowd of paparazzi, cameras ready.

"They're not here for *me,* although my new 'do *is* worthy," Mina said. "It's got to be that photo of you and Cabe." Mina, of course, had seen the photo as soon as it went viral. She'd seen it right before Mom and Dad confiscated her phone for ditching Mom yesterday to go to the movies with Rehann. For Mina, her phone was like an extra limb, and without it, she'd spent last night pacing our bedroom and plotting ways to get it back, without any success. "Face it, Sheyda. The world wants to know who his mystery girl is."

"I'm not his mystery girl!" I practically shouted. "I'm not his anything! And I'm the antithesis of mysterious! I'm . . . I'm average!"

Mina glanced at me, and for a second, her smirk softened into the smile of the sister who used to sneak me chocolate after lights-out and cuddle with me in bed when I got scared of the dark. She brushed a tangled strand of hair from my eyes. "Don't sell yourself short," she said. "You're anything but."

I would've smiled if I hadn't felt so nauseous. As I watched from the window, our neighbor Mr. Luccio appeared on the stoop with his pug, Dante, and was instantly accosted with questions. "Poor Mr. Luccio," I whispered. "He can't even take Dante for his morning walk." I spun to face Mina. "I can't deal with this. If they recognize me, they'll follow me to school, Doughlicious . . . everywhere! What am I going do to?"

"We'll make sure no one recognizes you." Mina opened our closet, tossing me outfits. They were all hers. Even though she was older than me, I was already as tall as she was, and we were about the same size. Still, Mina's ripped jeans and cool band

T-shirts were a far cry from my jewel-toned cardis and skirts. When I gave Mina a doubtful glance, she glared at me, hand on her hip. "Look. Do you want to get out of here without setting off more social media hysteria or not?"

Enough said. I put on her clothes, then let her sweep my hair into a knot and cover it with her favorite purple newsboy cap. Then she handed me a pair of her sunglasses.

"It'll work long enough to get you out the door," she said.

I sighed with relief. "Thanks."

She nodded and grabbed her backpack. "I've got to go. Mom's taking me early to meet with Mrs. Schafer. To discuss what sort of English assignments I might find 'intriguing.'" She grimaced.

I laughed, and sat down on the edge of the bed, trying to gather the courage for some honesty. "Can't you just . . . try fake liking it, at least?"

"Why? How I feel is how I feel, and I hate the conformity of class work. Like we're all worker bees cloning each other's ideas. Where's the originality?"

"Maybe you used it all up on your hair," I teased, and then we both cracked up.

"I just mean," I continued, "that they're asking you what you *want* to work on. They're only trying to help, so maybe . . . cut them some slack?"

She snorted. "*Me* cut *them* some slack? That's funny." She shook her head. "You don't get it. You don't even have to study and you still make the grades."

"I study," I protested. "I just don't blow it off."

Mina stared at me now. The angry smirk was back. "Forget it. I shouldn't have even said anything. I should've guessed you'd side with Mom and Dad."

"What? But—"

She was gone, slamming the door behind her.

I'm not siding with anyone, I wanted to yell after her. It wouldn't do any good, though. Just when I'd felt connected to her for the first time in months, when I'd caught a fleeting glimpse of the old Mina, she was gone again.

*   *   *

By the time I got to school, I was exhausted enough to feel like the entire day should already be over. Or the entire week, for that matter. After explaining (over and over and *over* again) to Mom and Dad how a harmless photo had spurred a media feeding frenzy, I'd escaped our apartment building miraculously unnoticed and unphotographed. I thought the worst of it was behind me and started to smile when I found Cabe waiting for me at my locker. Then I saw his grim expression, and my stomach sank.

"I should never have come with you yesterday," he said flatly. He ran a hand through his already-tousled hair. "This is the sort of thing that happens."

"It's crazy. There were reporters camped outside my door this morning—"

"What?" His eyes narrowed. "Did you talk to them? Because if you told them something was going on between us—"

"I didn't say a word!" I blushed with a combination of embarrassment and anger, then gestured to my outfit. "I didn't even leave the house until I made sure no one would recognize me." I glared at him as my head spun. "What do you think, that I wanted them taking more pictures?"

He stared at me suspiciously. "Maybe. For all I know, you could've planted that photographer in the donut shop."

I gaped at him. "I thought you'd know by now that I wouldn't do something like that." I grabbed my books out of my locker, suddenly wanting to be at my desk in first period with nothing more to worry about than my morning math quiz. "I don't even like posing for my yearbook pictures!"

"How do I know whether to believe you or not? You could be lying."

I gritted my teeth. That was the last straw. "I. Don't. Lie." I hoisted my bag onto my shoulder. "You know what? I hate that this is happening, because hanging out with you yesterday was . . . was fun." I swallowed, not quite believing I'd just admitted that. Then my mouth opened again, giving me another shock. "I thought maybe you had fun, too, but I guess I was wrong."

With my face burning and my heart racing, I turned on my

heel and walked away. I was so busy fuming that I didn't hear Kiri calling my name until I nearly slammed into her. She took one look at my face and dragged me into the girls' bathroom.

"Start talking," she said, and that was all it took for me to spill every horrific detail of the morning so far. When I'd finished, she shook her head. "I was afraid this might happen after yesterday."

I sighed. "I can't believe Cabe's accusing me of staging the whole thing. It's like he doesn't know me at all."

"Well, does he?" Kiri dabbed on some lip gloss. "He only just met you a couple of weeks ago. He probably doesn't have a clue who he can trust here."

"We're supposed to shoot the next scene for *Donut Go Breaking My Heart* after school today. What am I going to do if he's not talking to me? It'll be so awkward."

Kiri snapped her fingers. "I know what we'll do! I'll pull him aside during lunch so we can talk one-on-one. I'm sure I can get him to calm down."

I hesitated. Kiri had a history of coming to my rescue like this, and normally I accepted with gratitude. Once, in elementary school, she'd even told my version of what happened when I'd witnessed a fight between two other kids and had been called to the principal's office for questioning. I wasn't sure how I felt about her going to Cabe for me though. I wanted to be brave enough to face him on my own. Because it mattered to me. Because . . . *he* was starting to matter to me. "I can track him down between my classes," I started, but Kiri waved the idea away.

"Why should you stress?"

"Well, I could really use the extra time during lunch period to work on my model . . ."

"There you go. Now it's yours." The bell rang then, and we headed for the bathroom door. "Leave everything to me! I've got it covered."

"Okay," I mumbled. But I had that same disappointed quiver in my stomach that I'd had back in second grade in the principal's office, listening to Kiri tell *my* version of the story. The feeling that if I could only be braver, I wouldn't have to stand so often in Kiri's shadow.

The second Kiri walked into the makeup trailer after school, I jerked my head up so fast that I nearly got stabbed in the eye with a mascara brush.

"You must be still!" the makeup assistant warned. I nearly nodded but caught myself just in time.

"Did you talk to him?" I asked, trying to move my mouth as little as possible lest I incur the assistant's wrath again.

Kiri smiled and plunked down in the swivel chair beside mine. "Everything's fine. He wasn't even mad at you."

"He wasn't? It sure seemed that way."

"It really had nothing to do with you." My curiosity grew at that, but she didn't elaborate. "Anyway, the details don't matter. What matters is . . ." She clasped her hands together in excitement. "He was on the verge of really opening up to me. But he had to leave to meet with one of his teachers. He feels like I get him, you know?" She sat back with a satisfied sigh. "He brought up his movie premiere again. I think maybe it was a hint, so I told him I didn't have any Valentine's plans."

I squirmed in the chair, and the assistant yanked back the blush brush, frowning. "Sorry," I mouthed, then to Kiri I added, "So . . . you're going to go with him?"

"If he asks, of course I will! There will probably be talent scouts all over the place that night. *You* don't want to be his mystery girl, but I'd grab the chance in a second."

A knot formed in my throat. "So . . . you like him for real now?"

"Maybe." She smiled and stood up. "And we have our history project. That's the perfect way to fall 'in like.' We're working on it tonight after filming wraps up."

"Good," I said. "That's all . . . great." So why did I feel so incredibly lousy about it? And why was it that, for all Kiri's gushing over her hopes for 'falling in like,' there was something in her tone that nagged at me, something that rang insincere? "Kiri, just don't . . ." I tripped over my tongue. "Don't mess with him. He's a nice guy, so if you don't really like him, then—"

"Of course I won't!" She rolled her eyes. "Give me some credit!"

Mrs. Seng popped her head into the trailer door. "Kiri! There you are! What do you think? The donuts are just going to arrange themselves on tables?"

"I wish," Kiri mumbled.

Mrs. Seng glared at her. "Sheyda will go down to Donut Planet for me without complaint, but you? You grouse over everything."

Then Mrs. Seng was gone, leaving Kiri staring after her, irritation simmering on her face. "She'll never get me. She would've been happier having *you* for a daughter."

"She never means what she says," I said gently.

Kiri shook her head. "Sometimes I think she does." The comment sat between us with a new and strange awkwardness. I wrestled with trying to understand it, but then Kiri broke the silence with a glum, "I'll see you after you're done filming."

Once the trailer door clicked shut, I sat back in the chair. I wished Mrs. Seng wouldn't always compare me to Kiri. I wished

I'd tracked Cabe down at lunch and talked to him myself. I wished I could've been working on my model right now instead of prepping for an afternoon of camera lenses. I wished a lot of things that didn't have any hope of coming true.

"Okay," Jillian said from her director's chair, "are you two comfortable?"

No! I wanted to shout. I gave Cabe a quick side glance. He was staring at the floor. We were standing behind the counter at Doughlicious, about to shoot our scene. I was full of dread.

"So," Jillian continued, flipping through the script in her lap, "Marie and Prince Dalton are talking about the school dance, and Marie asks him if he's going to invite anyone. She's trying to figure out whether he likes Tia or not, but he's trying to avoid the question. You're both getting frustrated."

Well, that won't be a long shot, I thought. The set fell silent, the cameras began rolling, and Jillian called "Action!" I started stocking the glass display with donuts the way Jillian had instructed me to.

"You know the Winter Formal's only two weeks away," I recited from memory, feeling nervous. "Brian asked Tia if she would go with him."

Cabe, playing Dalton, frowned. "Did she say yes?"

"Not yet," I said. "There's someone else she's been hoping might ask her. Someone like you?"

Cabe fussed with the display. "She shouldn't get her hopes up about me. I'm not the guy she thinks I am. My life is . . . complicated. She wouldn't understand."

Ha! That sounded familiar. "I bet she would," I countered. "*If you took the time to be honest with her. You can't expect her to read your mind.*" Oops, that wasn't in the script! I'd just blurted it out. I waited for Jillian to call "Cut!" but she was gesturing madly to keep the cameras rolling.

"What if she doesn't like the truth?" Cabe asked.

"Don't you think you should let her decide that for herself?" I was way off script now, but I couldn't stop. "You're not being fair. You're shutting her out without giving her a chance."

His eyes widened in surprise, and he opened his mouth to

respond. "Hang on a second, Sheyda—er, I mean, Marie . . ." He blushed, waving his hand at the cameras to stop shooting. "Sorry! I blew it."

"No!" Jillian shot up from her chair. "That was good. Sheyda, I can see how nervous the cameras make you."

"I know," I admitted. "It's hard . . ."

"Just keep trying. Hopefully it'll get easier. In the meantime, you two are better together when you're off script, and we've got what we need for now. Let's take a ten-minute break."

I relaxed as the crew sprang into motion, adjusting lighting and moving cameras to set up for another scene. Cabe was instantly surrounded by his team of makeup artists, one of them muttering to him, "I've never seen you perspire like this. Since when do you get nervous? We're going to need more powder, people!"

Cabe's eyes flicked to my face, and I thought I detected a blush deepening across his cheeks. My heart raced, and I ducked my head, looking for a distraction. That's when I noticed Jillian watching a playback of the scene we'd just finished on her laptop. I inched closer and she waved me over.

"Take a look." She handed me her headphones. "Tell me what you think."

I slid on the headphones as she restarted the clip. It gave me a strange, out-of-body sensation, watching myself on the screen. I'd thought for sure I'd look like a complete novice. I *did* have a *deer-in-headlights* expression in my eyes, and I mumbled some of my words. Still, I wasn't nearly as stiff or awkward-sounding as I'd feared. There was another problem, though.

I pointed to the screen. "That napkin dispenser is distracting. Cabe looks like he's talking to it instead of to me."

Jillian nodded. "You're right. I was just thinking the same thing. We'll have to edit it out." She smiled at me. "You've got a good eye."

"Thanks." I blushed. "I love set design. It's what I want to do. Well, what I'm *trying* to do." I told her about my plan to apply for the design camp at NYU.

"No more acting in your future?" Jillian asked.

I shook my head. "I think everyone can tell it's not for me. But," I added quickly, "it's more interesting than I thought it would be."

Jillian laughed. "Hey, you're hanging in there, and we'll be done shooting before you know it. In the meantime, don't be shy about sharing design thoughts. Why don't you come early for Sunday's shoot? You could work with Trish, our set designer, for a bit, maybe get some pointers. And if you show Trish and me your plans for your model, I'll consider writing you a recommendation for the program."

I felt a rush of joy. "Really? Thank you, Jillian! That would be so great!"

She glanced over my shoulder. "Um . . . but now I think somebody might be waiting to talk to you." I turned to see Cabe a few feet away, trying to seem very involved with something on his cell phone but doing a horrible job of looking convincing. I nearly laughed. It was the first bad acting performance I'd ever seen him give.

I decided I'd be brave, so I took a few steps toward him. "Hey. I think I might've thrown you off during the scene."

"No worries. If Jillian says it worked, then I'm happy." He paused, still fiddling with his phone. "Sheyda, I'm sorry. About this morning. I've gotten into a horrible habit of assuming the worst of people. Paparazzi paranoia, I guess. And I took it out on you, which wasn't cool."

"Thanks," I said. "The truth is that this media storm is my worst nightmare. I'd never seek it out on purpose."

He nodded. "Yeah. Kiri said that at lunch today, too. But I should've listened to you this morning."

"I was only trying to tell you that . . . you don't have to worry about that with me."

"Ouch." He laughed softly. "So the idea of being my mystery girl is that repulsive, huh?"

"No! Of course not!" My face was blazing now. "I'd love to be your girl—" Omigod, WHAT?!? "I mean, I didn't mean . . ." I was going to die of humiliation. Right here. Right now. "I only meant that I'd never fake it for fame." I sneaked a peek at him, thinking he'd look horrified. Instead, he was grinning. "If I liked you, it would be for real," I added softly. "That's all."

"Good—I mean—I'm glad you're, um, for real." He looked up at me from under his long, dark lashes. "There aren't a lot of people I can trust. But I'm glad Kiri set things straight."

I nodded. "She looks out for me."

He tilted his head, studying me. "Maybe you don't need looking out for as much as you think you do. You didn't need to send her—"

"I didn't send her. She volunteered." Suddenly, I saw a chance to put in a good word for Kiri. "She's been your biggest fan since, well, forever."

He smiled. "I kind of got that impression," he whispered. "She's nice, but man, can she talk. If I hadn't had to leave for my meeting with Mr. Baldwin, she might still be going."

"That's Kiri." I laughed but felt baffled. The way he was talking about Kiri, it didn't sound like he was falling for her. I felt a strange surge of hope, followed instantly by a stronger surge of guilt.

"Cabe, Sheyda, we're ready for the next scene." Jillian's assistant was calling us over.

Cabe nodded, then turned back to me. "So if we're going to be friends, we'll tell each other the truth. I promise I won't doubt you again, and you promise to come to me yourself when you need to talk to me." He held out his hand, waiting for me to shake on it.

"I promise." I slipped my fingers into his. It could've been my imagination, but our hands seemed to rest against each other a little too long, until it felt like less of a handshake and more like hand holding. My breath caught as Cabe slid his hand away, but for the rest of the afternoon, I thought I could still feel the lingering warmth from his fingertips brushing mine.

Chapter Seven

I pressed the last step into place on my model staircase, careful to keep the glue from oozing over the sides. Then I sat back in my chair, stretching. I had to be at Doughlicious for filming by eight a.m., so I'd set my alarm for five to get up and work on my model.

"It's Saturday, for crying out loud," Mina had grumbled when my alarm went off. She still hadn't earned her cell phone privileges back, and it was making her extra grouchy. I'd instinctively reached for the switch on my desk lamp, ready to turn it off for fear of making her mad. But then I'd stopped myself.

"This is the only time I have," I'd said to her. I nearly added a "sorry," but held it in. The fact was, I didn't have anything to be sorry for. If Mina could keep me awake blaring music so loudly that even her earbuds couldn't contain the sound, then I had every right to work on my model. Mina grumbled some more, but eventually, amazingly, she got out her English assignment and started reading.

"What do you think?" I asked her two hours later, gesturing to the miniature spiral staircase I'd created. It was for the futuristic part of the *Romeo and Juliet* set. I'd designed it to be suspended from the stage's ceiling to give it the appearance of floating. Once the glue was dry, I was going to spray paint the stairs gold-and-red.

Mina inspected the staircase from all angles, the scowl on her face momentarily disappearing. "It's fantastic, Sheyda," she said sincerely. "You're so talented. Really."

I smiled at her, feeling a warm glow. "Thanks, but you don't have to say that."

"Believe me, I know I don't. Sometimes, it really peeves me that you're so creative."

"What?" I almost laughed, thinking she had to be joking, but I saw from her expression that she meant every word. I was shocked that she was being so honest. My hopes lifted. Maybe we could finally stop tiptoeing around each other and get into our sister comfort zone again. "You've always had more friends than me. You're braver, and cooler, and . . ." I shrugged.

"It's not about that." Mina flipped absently through the pages of her English book. "Do you know one of the best things about hanging out with Rehann and Josh?"

I shook my head.

She gave a small smile. "They don't really know you," she said, "so they can't make any comparisons." She sank back onto the bed. "Going skiing with them will let me blow off so much steam. Mom and Dad won't be hovering 24/7, and I can relax and be myself, you know?"

"But . . . you can't go on the ski trip."

Mina blinked, then nodded vehemently. "I *know*." She dropped her eyes to the floor. "I was talking hypotheticals."

There was a sudden tap on the bedroom window, and Rehann appeared on the fire escape, waving at Mina. "Are you coming?" Rehann mouthed to Mina.

Mina nodded and grabbed her hat and coat from the closet.

"Where are you going?" I demanded.

"Wouldn't you like to know?" Minas's eyes flashed impishly as she threw open our bedroom window. "One of us should be having some fun, so . . ." She grinned. "I'm happy to take one for the team. And don't you dare tell Mom and Dad anything!" She climbed through the window with Rehann's help, and then the two of them disappeared down the fire escape.

I shut my eyes. This was not good. Neither one of us was ever allowed to go anywhere in our neighborhood without our cell phones. I thought about telling Mom and Dad she'd left, but then Mina would know that I'd ratted her out. She'd never speak to me again if I did that. Besides, I thought as I checked the clock, I was supposed to be at Doughlicious for the filming in a little while. I'd just hope that Mina stayed out of trouble. She'd never done anything really risky any other time she'd snuck out. She wouldn't now. Would she?

When I got to Doughlicious I went in search of Jillian. She'd asked me to come early to meet with Trish, but now my heart thrummed with jitters. What if I did something stupid and blew my chance to impress her?

I found Jillian and Simeon watching in frustration as Trish and the prop assistants scurried about like ants, carrying all manner of donuts, chairs, and tables. The dining part of the shop was practically gutted, leaving only black-and-white-checkered flooring and the pink booths.

"Whoa." I surveyed the wreckage that used to be Doughlicious. "Mrs. Seng is going to freak when she sees this."

"Never you mind dear Mrs. Seng," Simeon said. "I knew she wouldn't be able to handle this, so the studio's paying for her to have a spa day. She's being wrapped in seaweed and bliss as we speak."

I laughed. "Is Kiri with her?"

Simeon frowned. "Poor girl's on donut duty. She's been handing them out to the crew since dawn. And pouting. She really does nail tween angst. It hasn't gone unnoticed."

"Really? So maybe she has a shot at some roles?"

"Ah, ah, ah." Simeon waggled his finger at me. "All I will say is"—he nodded toward Jillian—"the powers that be are watching."

"That would be so great for her. Donuts aren't her MO."

"Understood. And I'd be sympathetic, if I weren't dealing with this travesty." He swept his arm across the room. "A royal ballroom, it is not."

I looked at him blankly. "Huh?"

"You're teaching Cabe how to dance today," Jillian reminded me. "Cabe, or Prince Dalton, would only know formal ballroom dancing, right? But he's about to take Tia to the school dance. So

Marie"—Simeon pointed at me—"is going to teach him to dance, as practice."

My cheeks flushed. I'd forgotten that moment in the script. Dancing together meant being close to Cabe . . . really close.

"Sheyda?" Simeon was staring at me with a slightly amused, quizzical expression, as if he were trying to work out a puzzle. "Okay?"

I could only nod.

"But we're having a problem working with this narrow room," Jillian said.

Trish, the set designer, added, "We wanted to give you two as much floor space as possible, but the light in here's way too harsh, and the counter gets in the way of everything. We don't know how we're going to frame this shot."

I looked around and felt my mind shifting into design mode. After studying the sparseness of the room for a few seconds, inspiration struck. I took a deep breath and risked saying, "Maybe now there's too much space?"

Trish raised an eyebrow. "Explain?"

"Well . . . this isn't in a royal ballroom, so we should play up the clutter."

Trish gestured around the room. "Show me."

Heart racing, I grabbed one of the donut platters from a passing assistant and set it back on the display counter. I kept going, setting up a tower of donuts near the cash register.

"Good start," Trish said. "I'm thinking we add tables and chairs, too. See how the room seems unbalanced now?" I nodded, and we carried a couple of tables and chairs back into the dining area.

I hurried to the cleaning closet and returned with a mop and bucket. "If it's closing time, Marie and Dalton would be cleaning," I said. "While they danced, they'd be bumping into tables and chairs, or maybe knocking over the mop leaning against the wall."

As I talked, my insecurity faded. Trish gave me suggestions, pointing out some pitfalls we needed to avoid with the cameras, things I never would've thought of on a theater's stage. I started to get a sense of how different movie sets could be from drama sets, and how much I had yet to learn. It was eye-opening and exciting.

Within a few minutes, the shop had taken on the chaotic feel of closing time, complete with a stack of dirty dishes behind the counter and washrags resting on tables. I stood back, scanning the room for anything amiss.

"Bravo you," Simeon said, and I glanced up, startled out of my intense focus. Jillian and Trish were nodding in approval.

"This is just what the scene needed," Jillian said. Cabe, too, had walked in at some point while I was working, and now he was smiling at me in appreciation.

"Makeup's looking for you," he said. "But you've been busy. Teaching everyone a thing or two about set building, huh?"

I shrugged, blushing. "With a lot of help from Trish." Trish smiled at me. "It's not a big deal."

Simeon overheard me and tsk-tsked. "*Au contraire, cherie.* When you save the studio time, you save it money. And you've just helped save us at least an hour. Don't downplay it. Own it!"

I smiled, then hurried toward the door, mumbling, "I better get to makeup."

"Modest to a fault, that one," Simeon said to Cabe. "But lovely. Don't you agree?"

Cabe caught my eye, but I spun on my heel and was out the door before I could hear his response. I pressed my palms into my cheeks, trying to cool them down. What was happening? The way Cabe had looked at me just then? Had he been about to agree with Simeon? What if he had? My luck felt too impossibly good, Cabe's glance too impossibly encouraging.

I tried not to think about it as makeup and wardrobe poked and prodded, spraying stray hairs into place and coating my face with powder. But twenty minutes later, when I walked back into the shop, I felt a fresh burst of nervousness. This time it had nothing to do with set design, but everything to do with Cabe. His eyes found me the second I stepped through the door. I told myself I had to be imagining it, but as Jillian set us up for the scene, I kept feeling his glance. The second I looked his direction, though, his eyes would shift.

Finally, Jillian signaled that we were ready to begin filming, and we took our designated spots. The cameras began rolling, and I managed to get out my first line: "So, are you ready for the dance tomorrow night? Tia's excited."

"Absolutely!" Cabe said, exuding confidence in his Prince Dalton character. "Any princ—I mean, any person can dance." I nearly laughed at the cheesiness of that line from the script, but caught myself in time. "What, you think I'm bluffing?" Cabe asked teasingly, then took my mop and leaned it against the wall. "Here. I'll show you."

Cabe bowed formally. My job was to keep a straight face for at least a few seconds, which was difficult when he took my hand and began waltzing stiffly around the room with me in that old-fashioned way I'd seen people do in Jane Austen movies. Our outstretched arms formed a square of space between us, and our backs and heads were rigid. We bumped into two tables, then knocked over one of the chairs. That was my cue to break away from him, laughing.

"That's perfect," I said between giggles, "*if* you're attending a ball in Buckingham Palace."

Cabe looked indignant. "I thought that was how everyone danced?"

"Not quite." I smiled at him, but already my heart was racing at what the script said I had to do next. "Here. Let me show you."

I took his hands and placed them on my waist, then put my hands on his shoulders. "When you dance with Tia, you dance closer," I said softly, barely able to eke out the words over my roaring pulse. "Like this."

Simeon's iPhone began playing a ballad, and I led Cabe in a slow dance, swaying in time to the music. I knew that background music would be dropped into the film later on, but for now the phone was how we kept the beat. We moved in a small circle, navigating to avoid knocking into booths or chairs.

I took a breath, hardly believing I had to say the next line. "And you don't look at the ground when you dance with her. You look right into her eyes so that she knows that you're only thinking of her."

"Like this?" Cabe asked.

My heart bounded as he locked his eyes on mine. I nodded weakly. I could get lost in those eyes; staring into them was like swimming through a warm blue ocean. The rest of the room fell away, until it was just the two of us.

"This is . . . nice," he whispered.

His arms tightened around me, pulling me closer. His chin grazed my forehead. My eyes instinctively began to close, and for one breathless second, I thought he was leaning toward me, and my face lifted to meet his . . .

"Cut!" Jillian's voice was a wall rising up between us, and instantly we pulled apart, dropping our hands, clearing our throats, and looking everywhere but at each other. A few curious whispers flitted around the room, and a couple of the assistants giggled behind their hands. Were they whispering about me and Cabe, about what had just happened? I blushed. What *had* just happened? Nothing. Of course nothing.

"That was great," Jillian said briskly as she swept by with her laptop and a slew of assistants.

"It was," Simeon seconded. "You two are a regular Fred Astaire and Ginger Rogers." He leaned toward Cabe, adding, "Easy on the charm, though, Prince Dalton. You've got to save *some* for Tia."

My blush deepened, and the color rose in Cabe's face, too.

"Simeon's right," a familiar voice said, and I turned to see Kiri at my shoulder. "Tia's the love interest," she added to me. "You're the friend." Her smile was thin, wavering. She looked from me to Cabe and back again. "Sheyda, did you tell Cabe that he's the first guy you've ever danced with?"

I avoided Cabe's eyes. "School dances make me—"

"So nervous!" Kiri finished for me. "I've caught her hiding in the bathroom a few times."

"Kiri . . ." It might've been true, but she didn't have to overshare. Irritation burbled inside me. Not once in the entire time we'd been friends had Kiri ever truly ridiculed my shyness. I blurted, "Maybe I just want to do things in my own time, on my own terms."

My voice was hard, and Kiri's eyebrows shot up, but I kept going. "Maybe I've never wanted to dance with anybody before." *Oh no. No, no, no!* Had I actually said that? In front of Cabe? I snuck a glance at him. He looked surprised, but there was an amused smile playing at the corners of his mouth.

"I mean," I stammered, trying to backpedal. "Of course our dance was acting. And you're nice to dance with, but I wasn't saying . . . I didn't mean—"

"Breathe, Sheyda," Kiri interrupted. "We got what you meant. You're only a wallflower when you choose to be."

I stared at her. This was mean-girl talk; not at all like the Kiri I knew and loved. My anger boiled fresh.

Cabe's cell rang. Glancing at its screen, he said, "My manager's calling. I'll be back in a sec."

As soon as he was out of earshot, I turned to Kiri. "What's going on?"

She shrugged, focusing on her toes. "I don't know what you mean."

"I mean the way you're talking about me."

She stared at me, and then her pursed lips sagged. "I'm sorry. I don't know what's wrong with me today." She frowned. "Yes. I do. Donuts! I'm so sick of them! I spent all morning passing out donuts and coffee in the freezing cold, and you were in here . . ." She lowered her voice. "Dancing with the guy of *my* dreams!"

Ohhhhhhh. "It was just a dance, Kiri. Part of the script."

"Yeah? Well. It looked like more."

In a flash, I remembered the way Cabe's hands had felt around my waist, how being so close to him had swept my breath away. As I stood there debating what, if anything, to tell Kiri, Cabe walked back over to us. Kiri turned her attention to him, and I felt a tangible relief at being let off the hook.

"Let me guess." Kiri gave him a killer smile. "Your manager landed you a lead in a new movie. This one about macarons."

Cabe laughed. "No, but there's a Broadway producer that's considering me for a role in his new musical. He's given me tickets and VIP backstage passes to *Wicked* for tomorrow night. Have either of you seen it?"

We both shook our heads. "It's supposed to be fantastic," Kiri said longingly.

"Why don't you come with me to the show?" he suggested.

He'd barely gotten the words out before Kiri was gushing, "I'd love to!"

I smiled, even though my stomach dipped in disappointment. "You just made her day," I said to Cabe. "She's been dying to see *Wicked* for years."

He grinned at me. "I meant *both* of you. I've got three tickets."

"Oh," Kiri and I said together. There was a beat of silence.

"I'll check with my parents," I said, "but I'm sure they'll say yes." My heart hummed happily.

"After the show's over, we'll get to meet the cast and tour the set." Cabe looked directly at me when he said the last part. "I thought you'd like seeing it. It might help you with your model."

"I'd love to see it," I said. "Thanks." How sweet was it that he'd thought of that! But then I checked myself, trying not to read anything into it. He was just being friendly. That was all.

"Omigod, wait until I tweet this . . ." Kiri was already pulling out her phone.

"Actually," Cabe said, "I'd love it if you didn't. We'll have private balcony seats, and my manager's working with the theater's security so that I can keep a low profile. I'd like to see the show without a media storm. If that's okay."

Disappointment flashed over Kiri's face. "Sure!" she said, a little too cheerily. "I completely get that. Mum's the word." She pocketed her cell, then glanced toward the window, groaning. "Mom's back. I better go." She gave Cabe one lingering smile before she blew out the door.

We stood together, looking after her.

"Does she always do that to you?" Cabe asked quietly.

"What?"

"What she did before, talking about the school dances. It was like she was trying to make you feel small."

"No!" I protested. "She's never like that." I shifted my feet uneasily. "You have to know her the way I do. She's just having an off day."

He nodded. "Well, for the record, you're a great dancer." He blushed and smiled. This smile didn't exude celebrity confidence. It wasn't suave or centerfold-worthy. It was goofy, honest, and shy, and I loved every inch of it.

I couldn't help but smile back. "Thanks." In that second I knew for certain what my heart had been hinting at with its every racing beat. Forget common sense, forget my stubborn denial and my nonexistent chances. I was falling for Cabe, and that was a big problem.

Chapter Eight

"I don't see him anywhere!" Kiri said, leaning over the edge of the balcony and scanning the theater seats below us for any sign of Cabe.

I grabbed the waist of her skirt, just in case she leaned too far. "Kiri, he's coming. He told us he wouldn't get here until just before the show started. He doesn't want to draw anyone's attention, remember?"

I'd reminded Kiri of this at least ten times throughout the day, but she'd still insisted on having Mrs. Seng drop us off at the theater a whole forty minutes before curtain. I didn't mind leaving early for the theater, though. It meant forty minutes to live inside my head with Cabe. What I hadn't mentioned to Kiri was that Cabe and I had been texting since yesterday. He'd spent today exploring the city with his parents and had been giving me play-by-plays, complete with pics:

> Cabe: In Battery Park looking at Lady Liberty. BTW, why didn't you ever mention the glory that is a Sabrett's hot dog?

> Me: It's the element of surprise that I love best about NYC. Now try a hot pretzel w/ mustard.

> Cabe: Just did. Mind blown.

Then, an hour later:

> Cabe: There's a Marvel movie costume exhibit at the Met. I could totally pull off Iron Man.

> Me: Really? I had you pegged for a Captain America type.

> Cabe: Ouch. He's a wimp w/ a shield.

Me: LOL. Ok, Tony Stark. Didn't mean to bruise ur superhero ego.

Cabe: Where should I go next?

Me: Central Park. Check out the Delacorte Theater. There's free Shakespeare there every summer.

Cabe: Sounds cool.

Me: Outdoor stage. Starlight. To be or not to be. Need I say more?

Cabe: Nerd.

Me: Thank you. ☺

And so it went, until I felt like I'd spent the day with him (virtually, at least) in my city. It was fun, but not only that, the playful tone of his texts and his smiles in his silly selfies made me think he was having fun, too. Which meant that maybe he was starting to give Manhattan a real chance. And that meant maybe he would move here, and that meant I'd see him all the time, and that meant . . . putty. My heart was absolute putty at the thought.

"Sheyda?" Kiri's nudge broke through my daydreaming.

"Oh. Sorry." I blinked as I refocused on our spacious balcony seats in the Gershwin Theater. Once we'd handed an usher our VIP tickets, we'd been led up a back stairwell usually reserved as a fire exit. Then the usher had stocked us with snacks and drinks.

Now Kiri was eyeing me over her Milk Duds. "Where were you just now?" she asked, grinning. "Dreaming about your Romeo?"

I gulped. "Who? What Romeo?" Did she mean Cabe?

She shook her head, laughing. "Romeo and Juliet? Your set model?"

"Oh." Relief swept through me. "I guess so."

"Well, give your brain a break tonight. Okay? You deserve it." She said it so sincerely that I wanted to hug her. We'd been off lately, but maybe this was a sign we were back on track.

"Thanks," I said, then felt a stab of guilt. If only she knew who I'd really been thinking about.

"I could get used to this," she said, taking a sip from her Shirley Temple. "First-class treatment all the way." She fluffed her skirt, fidgeting nervously in a way that was completely out of character for her. "Are you sure I look okay?"

This was the hundredth time she'd asked. "You look gorgeous."

She did, too. She'd used every last cent of her allowance to buy a new outfit—a pastel pink chiffon skirt and cream sleeveless cowl-neck top. It made her look older and more sophisticated. I had to give her that. She could pull off glam as well as any celeb.

The outfit I'd originally chosen for myself had been more like camouflage. I'd gone with all black—every New Yorker's fail-safe ensemble. Kiri, though, had taken one look at me when I'd arrived at her house and whisked me into her bedroom, shaking her head. "I can't let you hang with Cabe Sadler in funeral garb."

Fifteen minutes later, I'd emerged from her bedroom in a crimson tunic, black leggings, and red booties. The whole outfit was bolder and brighter than anything in the realm of my comfort zone, but when I'd glanced in Kiri's full-length mirror, I'd been surprised, and cautiously pleased, with the result. The red color gave my skin a nice bronze glow, and Kiri had swept my thick black hair back into a braided half-updo.

Now, as I smoothed the tunic over my legs, the lights in the theater flashed a warning to the audience to take their seats. Just as Kiri was giving me another worried *he's-not-showing* look, a hand brushed my shoulder.

"Hey," Cabe whispered to us, taking the seat in between me and Kiri.

"You made it!" Kiri whisper-shrieked.

"Barely," he said. "We got stuck in Times Square traffic and I had to get out to make a run for it. I thought I saw someone snap a pic of me walking into the theater just now, but I won't know for sure until after the show. If there's a mob of reporters waiting for me outside the theater, that means the word got out."

"Oh, maybe our picture will make it into the *Times*," Kiri said excitedly, but when she noticed Cabe's grim expression, she added, "but that's probably just peanuts to someone as famous as you."

Cabe nodded at her, but his eyes, I noticed, kept returning to me.

"You look amazing," he whispered as the lights dimmed for good.

I heard Kiri respond with "thank you" before I could say anything, and I let it go. Still, I couldn't help wondering if his words had been meant for me. My heart skipped a few beats in hopefulness as the curtain lifted.

The orchestra played its opening chords, the stage lights illuminated the imaginative set below us, and the performers took their spots and began to sing and dance. I leaned forward, drawn to the edge of my seat by the excitement of the show. But all the while, I was keenly aware of Cabe's presence beside me. Every time he shifted in his seat, or rested his elbow on the arm of his chair, I longed to lean in closer to him.

By the time Elphaba and Glinda took their final bows, I was dizzy with adrenaline. We waited until the rest of the audience emptied the theater, and then a tour guide came to escort us backstage.

"Did you like the show?" Cabe asked me as we walked into the shadows of stage left. "I wasn't sure. You seemed distracted."

Ha. If he only knew. "I loved it," I said, but I'd barely gotten the words out when Kiri stepped between us, slipping her arm through Cabe's.

"My favorite part was when Elphie sang 'Defying Gravity,'" she said. "But that green stage makeup! The poor girl must've felt like she was suffocating under it. I bet her skin still looks green even after she wipes it off." She turned to the tour guide. "I'd love to know how you lifted Elphaba up over the stage for that song."

The tour guide smiled politely. "We use special wires and harnesses for that part of the show." He motioned for us to follow him onto the stage. "I'll show you how we do it."

Kiri led the way behind our guide, holding tight to Cabe's arm, and that was the beginning of half an hour of Kiri firing off question after question. As soon as the guide finished answering one, Kiri had another one ready. Two or three times, I tried to say something about the placement of the backdrops on the stage and about the construction of the cages for the flying monkeys. Kiri interrupted each time.

I fell into step a few feet behind the three others, figuring that I had a better chance of exploring the set myself than I did trying to get the attention of the tour guide.

"Excuse me," Cabe said. "Everything you've told us so far is fascinating. But I think Sheyda would love to hear more about how the sets were designed and built. She's a set designer herself."

The tour guide glanced at me. "Is that so? A budding artist in our midst."

Cabe grinned at me while I blushed. *She's a set designer.* It was the first time in my life someone had ever called me that. Hearing Cabe speak it out loud had made it feel like less of a dream and more of a certainty.

"Well, most tourists only care about the chance to chat backstage with the performers," the guide said, "so this will be a treat for me." He walked us to center stage. "Eugene Lee, the set designer, used a clockwork theme." He motioned toward the giant cogs and wheels hanging high above our heads. "When he was brainstorming the set, he threw an old clock down some stairs, breaking it so that he could look at all its pieces."

I nodded. "I saw the picture of Eugene's set model on YouTube," I admitted sheepishly. "I'm kind of a set design geek." I glanced up at the enormous silver dragon looming above the stage. "The clockwork dragon is my favorite part."

"Mine, too," the guide said. "Do you know it's made of foam? The whole thing weighs less than forty pounds."

"That's amazing." I stared at it, awestruck by the magic of the illusion it created. That was why I loved set design so much. You could take simple materials and make something incredible to capture an audience's imagination.

I followed the tour guide to where the giant gold "floating head" sat in the darkness at the corner of the stage. "Go ahead. Take a look." He pointed me toward the complicated backdrop of wires and metal behind the head. "Can you guess how the prop hand might operate it?"

I stepped up to the panel and saw an odd foot pedal at its bottom and a hole in the center of the panel with a familiar-looking handle protruding from it. "Is that a . . . a bike brake handlebar?"

The tour guide smiled, nodding. "That's how you control the head, along with the bass drum pedal here." He gestured to the pedal on the floor. "Try it out."

My heart hammered with excitement as I experimented with pushing the pedal and squeezing the handlebars, making the gold head open and close its mouth and lift its eyebrows.

"I'm not really supposed to do this, but . . ." The tour guide flipped a few switches, and the head's eyes lit up and smoke poured from its nostrils.

"So cool!" I laughed. "Kiri, do you see this?"

I looked over my shoulder, waiting for her to respond. But I was met with only silence and the tour guide's worried gaze. "I thought they were right here. I hope they didn't wander too far," the guide said, turning the head off and walking toward the wings. "They're supposed to stay with me."

I followed the guide through a series of narrow hallways. When we neared a dressing room, we heard a commotion. We peered into the open door and found Cabe and Kiri surrounded by half a dozen *Wicked* performers, all still in costume. Kiri was seated in an armchair with her leg propped up on a stool. The cast members were offering her ice packs and fussing over her like she was mortally wounded. Cabe was seated on the arm of Kiri's chair, concern creasing his face.

"What did I tell you about those cables?" a costumed monkey was saying to the scarecrow. "Didn't I say someone was going to break a leg?"

"It's not broken," Kiri said, offering up a weak smile.

I squeezed into the huddle. "What happened?" I asked Kiri.

Her eyes turned glassy. "I feel like such a klutz. I tripped over a wire." She wiggled her right foot and winced. "I think I sprained my ankle."

A chorus of "poor thing" followed, along with a renewed offer from someone to fetch more ice. Kiri waved them away as she wrapped her ankle in a bandage someone had unearthed from a first aid kit. "Please, you all have done enough already. I'll be fine."

"We should get you back home," I said. "Your mom might want to take you for an X-ray."

"No," she groaned. "I don't want to cut our tour short." She tried to stand but sank back into the chair, grimacing. "Okay," she said meekly. "I give. You're right."

"I already called Ben for the car," Cabe said. "He's waiting outside the side exit."

Cabe slipped his arm around Kiri's waist to help her out of the chair. A path parted in the dressing room, and we slowly made our way to the exit, with Kiri apologizing all the way for causing so much trouble.

I opened the door a crack and a wave of deafening screams and chants of "Cabe! Cabe! Cabe!" hit me. Just before I slammed the door shut, I saw the flashes fire on about a hundred phones. "Um, you guys?" I pressed my back against the door. "We have a problem. There's a ton of reporters and fans out there."

Cabe frowned, but his expression was resolved. "It's okay. The only thing that matters right now is getting Kiri home safe."

Kiri squeezed his arm. "You're too sweet for words."

My stomach lurched as Cabe smiled down at her. *Get a grip,* I scolded myself. Here was my best friend, injured, and I was jealous of a little smile? I needed to be supportive, not possessive. I took a deep breath and when Cabe nodded, I opened the door again.

We stepped out into blinding flashes and cheers, and I instantly had to fight the urge to run back inside. How did Cabe deal with this? I took Kiri's other arm, trying to hurry her as much as was possible toward the curb and Cabe's waiting car. We took a few staggering steps, and then Kiri stopped.

"What's wrong?" I whispered.

She didn't respond, but slipped her arm from mine and stepped closer to Cabe. Then she offered up a fragile wave to the crowd. "Tonight, Cabe Sadler's my real hero!" she called. She beamed up at him, and then kissed him on the cheek.

My heart dropped to my toes as the fans exploded into

whistles and applause. Kiri's smile widened, while Cabe's expression was a turnstile of emotions. First embarrassment, next confusion, and then panic crossed his face. He double-timed it to the open car door with Kiri, and I did my best to keep up, clumsily spilling into the car after the two of them. Fans swarmed the limo, but Ben pulled away from the curb and into the stream of traffic in Times Square.

The multicolored lights beaming in from the windows showed Cabe tight-lipped and silent, staring into his lap, while Kiri sat back with a tired sigh.

"I hope I didn't ruin your night," she said to Cabe. "This is all so embarrassing." She gestured toward her ankle.

"Don't worry about it." He gave her a small smile.

I stared at Kiri. All I could think about was her kiss. *Their* kiss. How could she have done that in front of all those cameras, when she knew full well how closely Cabe was scrutinized?

When Cabe's cell rang, all three of us jumped.

"Hello?" Cabe's voice was tense, and within seconds, I'd guessed from all the "uh-huhs" and "oh nos" that this was not good news. After he hung up, he collapsed against the seat, pressing his fingers to his temples. "That was my manager. There's a photo of . . . of us." He glanced at Kiri, and I could see pink rising to his cheeks even in the dim light of the car. "Trending on Instagram. It's gotten ten thousand likes in five minutes." He swiped his thumb across his phone's screen, then handed it to me and Kiri.

There it was—a picture of Kiri kissing Cabe, her eyes gleaming in adoration as she gazed up at him. I could barely breathe as I looked at it. They were a beautiful couple, no doubt about it. Kiri hit the back arrow on the screen and a montage of photos of her and Cabe, all from various angles popped into view. Then there was another photo, showing Kiri and me, side by side. The caption screaming under the photo read: CABE TOO YOUNG FOR TWO CRUSHES?

I shut my eyes and turned away from the phone, feeling nauseous.

"I had no idea this would happen," Kiri said softly. "I only wanted to say thank you. I'm sorry."

"It's not your fault." Cabe sounded resigned. "It'll blow over." He tossed his phone onto the empty seat beside him.

We spent the rest of the ride sitting in stilted silence, and I was relieved when the car finally pulled up to Kiri's front stoop. Ben jumped from the car to help Kiri while I made sure I had Kiri's purse and coat, which I'd offered to bring inside.

I was about to climb out of the car but hesitated, turning back to Cabe. The shadows in the car turned his eyes into a midnight sky. He was trying hard to hide his frustration, but the effort was only making the muscles along his jawline clench even tighter. It made him look angsty, and—sigh—ridiculously cute.

"Will this be a huge problem?" I asked.

His phone started ringing again, but he turned it off. "You know what? It doesn't matter. I spent all day walking around town, and not a single person asked me for my autograph. You were right about that. New Yorkers really just leave each other be. I liked that. A lot."

"But the paparazzi? The fans who won't leave you alone?" I asked.

"They might always be around, but I'm done letting them get to me. Rumors aren't real, so why should I care? If I ever want to have a life outside of the spotlight, I need to learn to act like it doesn't exist." He looked at me, his expression serious. "But I'm sorry about how things ended tonight. I wanted it to be fun for you."

"I *did* have fun." I smiled. "It was amazing seeing the set and props. It was probably one of the coolest things I've ever done in the city."

He brightened. "Really?"

I nodded. "So . . . thanks." I set one foot out of the car, but Cabe touched my hand. "Sheyda. Wait." His hand was still over mine, and heat shot through my fingers. "I wanted to tell you—"

"Ready, miss?" a voice said, and I glanced up to see Ben extending his hand to help me out of the car. I glanced back at Cabe. "What?" I asked weakly, as all sorts of imaginings flitted through my mind. What was he going to say? That he liked Kiri, probably. But maybe . . . what if he liked me? What if he was about to say it out loud? My heart ached with hope, but I told it to chill. There was Kiri, first of all, and the impossibility of ever doing anything to hurt her. And then there was Cabe, a boy completely out of my league, practically out of my universe. It couldn't be.

Cabe sat back against the seat, the determination in his face fading. "I'll see you at school tomorrow."

My heart sank. *Good,* I told it. *Get used to it, because this is how things are.* "Yup," I said, my voice reaching for a lightness I didn't feel. "Tomorrow."

"Can I get you some more ice?" I asked as Kiri settled back onto her bed, her ankle resting on a mountain of pillows. She was already streaming her favorite Cabe Sadler movie on her tablet and sipping some hot chocolate Mrs. Seng had made for us.

"I'm good, thanks," Kiri said distractedly as she stared at the tablet's screen. She lifted it up to me for a glimpse. "He looks even better now than he did here, don't you think? Can you imagine how cute he'll be in high school?" She smiled, without a trace of the discomfort she'd had back at the theater.

"Does it still hurt?"

She glanced down at the ice pack encasing her foot. "Sure it hurts . . . Ooooh! This is the best part of the whole movie!"

Her cell phone buzzed. I spotted it on her desk just as Kiri jumped off the bed. "I've got it."

For a second, all I could do was stare. Kiri had a sprained ankle, but I'd just seen her leap out of bed with the enthusiasm of a gymnast, and now she was standing with her full weight on both feet, ogling her phone.

"Oh. My. God." Kiri hopped up and down. "Val just texted. She said the entire school's seen the photo of me and Cabe. And someone wrote a song about the two of us and posted it on YouTube."

"Kiri." It took all my effort to keep my voice calm. "Your ankle."

"Huh?" She glanced up, and then an instant later was hobbling back toward the bed. "Ow, ow, ow," she mumbled, her face twisting in pain. "I forgot."

I wanted to believe her. I *needed* to believe her. She'd been in tears at the theater. And pale, even. The pain had seemed so real! If she'd faked that . . . she was a good actress. Good enough to have fooled me. And Cabe.

I sat down on the bed and stared out the window, snapshots from our friendship flowing through my mind. Kiri picking my outfits for the first day of school; Kiri choosing where we sat in the cafeteria. Had I ever made a single decision on my own when the two of us were together? A slow burn started in my chest, and I felt words building up at the back of my throat that I'd never imagined saying. Like, *What are you doing?* And, *How could you?*

"Kiri," I started.

"Hmmm?" Kiri mumbled. She flopped forward to give me a spontaneous, sideways hug. "Hey, thank you so much for tonight." Her eyes were full of gratitude, but I wondered what it was gratitude *for.* Taking care of her after she hurt her ankle, or letting her stake a claim with Cabe? She squeezed my hand. "I couldn't ask for a better bestie."

The burning in my chest fizzled.

"You're welcome," I finally mumbled as Mrs. Seng walked into the room.

"Sheyda, I should walk you home," she said. "It's late."

I nodded and stood, checking the time. "Ugh. And I still have work to do on my model."

"Tonight?" Kiri asked in surprise. "It's almost eleven!"

"The *Donut* filming's been taking so much time, and the application's due in five days." I yawned. "It's going to be a late night."

Kiri shook her head. "You'll finish it on time. You've never turned anything in late in your life."

My anger flared again. I was getting sick of comments like that. From Kiri, Mina, my parents, my teachers. Just once, it might feel good for someone to be worried about me, instead of expecting me to handle everything the way I always did.

A few minutes later, as I walked through the quieting streets with Mrs. Seng, disappointment settled into my skin. Maybe Kiri *was* playing pretend, but wasn't I pretending, too? I hadn't had the courage to confront Kiri, and now I was doing what I'd done for as long as I could remember: pretending everything was okay.

I was letting myself down, and somehow, that made me feel even worse than the photo of Kiri and Cabe's kiss.

Chapter Nine

"I can't believe you told them!" Mina yelled as she barreled into our room Monday morning. I jerked upright in bed, startled out of a dreamless sleep. I'd stayed up until two in the morning working on my model, and now the whole world was taking on the fuzzy cast that came with exhaustion.

"What are you talking about?"

"You told them I snuck out on Saturday! And now I'm grounded for a whole month. You went behind my back. Unbelievable!"

"Mina, I don't know how they found out. I didn't say a word."

I stood up groggily. I'd gone to bed still angry over holding my tongue with Kiri, and now I felt everything building up inside me again.

Mina glared at me. "Yeah right. You just had to be Miss Perfect, didn't you?"

"Shut up!" I shouted. It came out so loudly that I shrank from the sound of my own voice. Mina's eyes saucered in shock, but I didn't care anymore. "Blame me if you want. You're the one who broke the rules, so . . . so just get over it!"

"Sheyda?" My mom came into the room wide-eyed and worried. "Was that you yelling? That's not like you."

"Aaaaaagh!" I cried in frustration. *Not like me.* "You don't know what's like me and what isn't! None of you have a clue." These days, *I* didn't even know!

I stormed into the bathroom to wash up, then got dressed quickly, throwing on a sweater over my leggings. As I grabbed my bag, I remembered there was a math test today. I'd been planning to study over the weekend, but with the filming and everything else, I'd completely forgotten.

"I'm going to school," I said. If I left now, maybe I could study at school before class started. I blew past Mina and Mom, who were still standing, frozen, in the center of the room. I vaguely registered the astonishment on their faces but ignored it. "Fight all you want. I'm so, so sick of it, and I don't have to stay here and listen."

If they said anything after that, I was out the door before I could hear it. I must've looked as volcanic as I felt, because when the paparazzi stationed outside saw me, they instinctively took a step back.

One brave reporter snapped a photo and blurted, "Sheyda, how do you feel about your best friend kissing Cabe Sadler?"

Ugh. If I'd had a rotten tomato, I would've launched it at his face. Instead, I took off at a jog down the street. The sky was heavy and the cold air felt good against my blazing skin, but that was the *only* thing that felt good today so far. A couple of minutes later, when I flew past Kiri's apartment, my step didn't falter. Today, I was going to school alone.

*   *   *

My mood didn't improve when I spotted more paparazzi hovering around the school. Before they saw me, I skirted around to the entrance that led into the theater. Once inside, I climbed the stairs to my hiding spot on the catwalk, trying to calm down. I wished I could hang out in the quiet darkness for the rest of the day. The idea of seeing Kiri, of having to pretend like I was okay, made me queasy. I pulled out my math textbook and, using my phone's flashlight, made a sorry attempt at studying. There wasn't a chance I could prepare for this test in an hour. I'd have to wing it, something I'd never done before, and hope I could at least pass.

I didn't know how much time had gone by before I heard a voice from below call out, "Sheyda?" I peered over the catwalk to see Ms. Feld on the stage, shaking a light dusting of snow from her lavender coat. "Is that you up there, *bubala*? The bell's set to ring in a couple minutes."

I made my way down the stairs as Ms. Feld flipped light switches, illuminating her office.

"There's quite a stir out front. A crowd of reporters waiting for our Mr. Sadler." She peered at me with curiosity, and I wondered if the rumors about Cabe and me and Kiri had managed to reach even her ears. I dropped my eyes, not sure what I'd do if she started asking questions. Ever since I'd left my apartment, I'd felt so close to tears that I was afraid even the littlest thing might start them falling. "It's just started snowing, and the forecast is predicting it will get heavier midmorning. There might be an early dismissal."

Not early enough, I thought, dreading my math test.

"So. Your model. You'll bring it in for me to see on Friday?" I nodded, and she smiled. "Feel free to bring it in earlier if it's finished. I can't wait to see it!"

My stomach flip-flopped. "You'll have it by Friday," I managed weakly, and then added, "I'd better get to class."

I hurried out into the bustling hallway, keeping my head down as I made my way to my locker. In my rush, I ended up smacking right into someone's shoulder.

I glanced up and a pair of ocean eyes met mine. "Oh. Hey, Cabe," I started, but then I stepped back, taking in the rest of the picture. Kiri, whose ankle was still wrapped in the bandage, had one arm around Cabe and the other holding a glittery hot-pink cane. Cabe was dressed up as Charlie Chaplin, and Kiri was wearing an old-fashioned twenties-style dress. Their costumes didn't make any sense to me until I remembered the history project they'd been working on together. Today must've been their day to present to the class.

"Sheyda!" Kiri cried. "Where were you this morning? I tried calling you a bunch of times." I shrugged. I'd silenced my phone while I was studying.

"Cabe offered to take me to school, and I wanted to tell you." She gave him the dewy-eyed look of a kitten being rescued from a tree. "Wasn't that sweet of him?"

"I was worried about her walking on that ankle," Cabe explained.

"He gave me this awesome cane, too! Maybe I'll start a new fashion trend with it."

"Yeah," I said flatly, and then to Cabe, "That was nice of you."

He cleared his throat as Kiri tightened her grip around him.

"We're giving our history presentation today. How embarrassing that I have to give it with everyone staring at my ankle." She rolled her eyes.

"Well. Good luck. I have to go . . ." I said, already moving past them. "I have a math test, but . . . see you later!" It was meant to sound breezy, but came out about as breezy as a bowling ball.

"Sheyda, wait . . ." Kiri called after me, but I didn't look back as I quickened my step. I was sure Kiri was wondering what was wrong with me, but where would I even start?

A few kids gave me longer-than-usual looks as I passed them in the hallway, and Phoebe and Val were waiting for me at my locker.

"Details, girl," Phoebe ordered. "What happened last night?"

"You saw the pictures" was all I could manage to say. I tried to shrug my shoulders, but my body was too rigid to cooperate. "They tell the story."

Val's forehead crinkled. "Are you okay?"

"Of course I am!" My heart sped up. "Why wouldn't I be?"

Val and Phoebe exchanged glances, and Phoebe nodded in response to some unspoken agreement between the two of them. "So don't freak, but we're worried about you. You've kept everything on the DL, but we thought maybe you and Cabe—"

"That me and Cabe what?" I snapped. "Me and Cabe nothing. We're . . . *nothing*, okay?"

Phoebe held up her hands. "Okay, Sheyda."

"I have to go," I said. "Test prep."

Their eyes stayed on me as I walked away, and I was sure they'd be texting me later. I didn't want to be so short with them, but I was emptied out of patience. All I wanted was to be left alone. By the time I sat down in class, I was so on edge I was trembling.

Snow was falling steadily outside the windows as Mr. Quinten handed out our tests. Once he gave the go-ahead, I flipped over the paper, and my heart plummeted. I had no idea what the answer to the first question was.

The test was a disaster, and I felt the doom of it long after I headed to my other classes. When Principal Gomez's voice crackled over the intercom to announce the early dismissal after third period, my spirits lifted for a second.

Then my cell buzzed with a text from Cabe: CAN YOU MEET AT DOUGHLICIOUS? NEED TO RUN THRU A SCENE. JUST YOU AND ME. IT'S LAST MINUTE, BUT YOU'D BE A LIFESAVER IF YOU SAID YES.

I remembered the last scene Cabe and I had filmed together: the dance. I wanted to have another moment like that. I'd been *hoping* for another moment like that. It was infuriating. It was irresistible.

OK, my fingers typed, before I even realized they were doing it. SEE YOU IN FIVE.

"You want me to what?" I stared at Cabe, collapsing into one of the Doughlicious booths. The shop was quiet, closed for the snow. Cabe had asked Mrs. Seng if we could have the space for an hour.

"Um . . . practice this scene with me?" Cabe said again as I stared at the script.

This scene only had one line, and it was Cabe's. That wasn't the problem. The problem was . . .

"But . . . it says we're supposed to . . . that we have to . . ." I swallowed. I couldn't even say the word: "kiss." There it was, in bold letters on the page.

Cabe's face was the exact shade of a Big Apple tour bus, and he couldn't meet my eyes.

"It's really only a quick peck on the lips, but . . . we don't have to do that part if you don't want to. I just want to make sure I know how to stand for the cameras."

"Why?" My heart was thrashing. "I mean, you've done scenes like this tons of times." Kiri was big on pausing Cabe's movies at kisses so she could admire his "perfect lips." And, yes, they *were* pretty perfect.

"I know, but Sonora Grace is flying in from LA late tonight."

"Who?" I asked blankly. I was only half listening, trying to pretend like this wasn't really happening.

"The actress who's playing Tia in the movie, aka the Wicked Witch of the West Coast?" Cabe sighed. "I've never had to work with her, but I've heard it's awful. She's stormed off sets before. Once she dumped an entire can of paint on her costar's head, just because he botched a kiss. She wants her role in the movie filmed in the next three days, and nobody wastes her time. So I've got make sure I get it right. We start filming her scenes tomorrow."

"You should ask someone else," I said softly. "I'm not sure—"

Cabe lifted his eyes to mine.

"The thing is . . . I get nervous." He stopped, swallowing. "But I never get that kind of nervous around you."

He looked so hopeful that I knew I'd do it, even if I was weak with nerves and crazy excitement. "Okay," I managed to reply. "Just . . . show me what I need to do."

He looked relieved. "Thanks," he said. He led me to our marks on the floor. "Sonora and I will both be standing here." Cabe put his hands around my waist, and my knees liquefied. "Come closer," he said, pressing his fingertips against the small of my back. "Closer."

We were standing so near each other now that I was sure Cabe could feel the beating of my heart. "So, just before we, you know, kiss, I say, 'No princess could ever be as important to me as you are.' That's our cue. All right?"

"Uh-huh," I squeaked. When I finally risked a look at him, he was frowning.

"Hey. You okay?" he asked quietly. "You don't seem like yourself today."

I gulped, my pulse roaring in my ears. "I'm f-fine."

"'Cause you actually look like you're really dreading this."

"Me?" My laugh twanged like a guitar string breaking. "No! No. I'm not. I mean, it's totally fine. I want to kiss you. I mean, I don't *want* to kiss you for real, but, but . . ." *Oh help.* "It's just I've never kissed anyone before." *What?!?* My mouth was being run over by a freight train of words, and what was coming out of it was the wreckage.

Cabe stared at me, and for one terrifying second, I thought he might laugh. But instead, he smiled, gently, kindly, unbelievably cutely. "Really? Well. Then . . . it's an honor."

I smiled, and my heart soared. It was the sweetest thing he could have said to me. The sweetest thing *any* guy had ever said to me. Cabe smiled and tucked a strand of hair behind my ear. Our foreheads were nearly touching, and my heart was melting.

"No princess could ever be as important to me as you are," he whispered. And suddenly the rest of the world was dropping away, because Cabe's lips were moving toward mine. Then they met mine, and the world stopped existing entirely.

His lips were *so* soft. It was good he was holding on to me, because otherwise I might have sunk straight into the floor with bliss. I wanted the kiss to last forever, but then, all too soon, Cabe was pulling away. The room came into sharper focus, and my face flamed. What if I was a bad kisser? What if I'd looked ridiculous? Or worse, what if I'd looked the way I felt, like I could've stayed there kissing Cabe Sadler forever?

I dropped my eyes self-consciously, but then I heard Cabe's soft "thank you" in my ear.

I looked up to catch his earnest gaze. Then the shop's door jingled.

"Hey, guys!" Kiri said, walking in and looking none too happy. "Sorry if I'm interrupting . . . something." Obvious emphasis on "something." "I forgot my bag in the kitchen. I'll only be a sec."

"We were just . . ." I lost my voice.

"Running through a scene," Cabe finished for me.

She hobbled past me, but then paused in front of Cabe. "That was some great acting. You made it look so real." She gave me a long, sharp look. "*Both* of you."

"Kiri, Cabe asked me to stand in for Sonora Grace," I started. "She's—"

"It was fake," Cabe said suddenly, with a nonchalant shrug. I watched as, in a matter of seconds, his whole demeanor shifted into casualness. "We only have to make it look real."

The cloud I'd been floating on evaporated, and I careened headlong into reality. Of course it had been fake. I was so naïve to think our kiss meant anything to him. Well. This was the perfect capper to my awful day. My eyes stung, and I blinked rapidly to stave off tears. I spun to grab my bag and coat.

"We're finished, right? Because I really need to get going—"

"Sheyda?" Cabe said as I hurried past him and Kiri.

I couldn't stop. Instead, I mumbled something about a headache and having to get home ASAP. I shut the door on their surprised faces and, flipping the hood of my jacket over my head, ducked into the falling snow. My phone buzzed in my pocket, and when I checked the screen, there were already three texts from Kiri asking what was wrong.

How could I answer without telling her the truth? How could I tell her the truth without destroying our friendship?

I pushed my phone deeper into my pocket and hurried on.

I didn't know how long I'd been sitting on my front stoop, but if the tingling in my fingers and toes was any indication, I'd have to go inside soon before frostbite struck.

Lucky for me, the snow had proved too much for the paparazzi, so no one was skulking outside our building. My phone kept buzzing, but I hadn't looked at it again. I couldn't deal.

I heard a car pull up to the curb, but didn't look up until I heard a familiar voice say, "*Excusez-moi, mademoiselle,* but might I offer you some shelter from the cold?"

I glanced up to see Cabe peering out of the window of his limo.

Pull it together, I thought as my heart triple-flipped. But what I said as I walked over to the car was, "Your French accent is terrible."

"Good thing I've never been cast in a French film, huh?" He laughed, then turned serious. "I got worried when you left in such a hurry. I thought that, um, well, when we, you know . . ."

Omigod. He meant when we kissed. My pulse raced.

"I thought it upset you. That I did something wrong."

"No!" I blurted. "It was fine. Just acting, right?"

"Right." He nodded. "Good. That's a relief." Funny, though. He didn't sound relieved. More like disappointed. He gestured for me to enter the limo, and I opened the door, climbing inside and waving hello to Ben. "Are you hungry?" Cabe asked.

"Um . . ." On cue, my stomach rumbled.

Cabe grinned, and some of the awkwardness between us vanished. "I'll take that as a yes." He picked up a pastry box from the seat beside him. "I brought you some *zoolbia bamieh* from Ravagh Persian Grill. The waiter who helped me told me they're like donuts?"

I couldn't help but grin. "Persian donuts, made with saffron and rosewater. So delish. And Ravagh's my favorite Persian restaurant. How—"

"Kiri mentioned it a while ago. The other food there looked and smelled incredible, too. And, they have takeout." He held up a menu. "This one's going on the top of my list. I mean, seriously, is there any food you can't get in this city?"

I nodded. "In-N-Out burgers."

He face fell. "So . . . I could have them flown in from LA."

I rolled my eyes. "And that doesn't smack at all of celeb-snob status."

He laughed. "Kidding! Just checking to make sure you're still keeping me in line."

"Always. And thanks. For the *bamieh*. Ravagh's the best. My family and I eat there every year for Nowruz." At his blank look, I added, "It's the Persian New Year to celebrate the start of spring. At Ravagh, they always serve the traditional New Year's meal, salmon and rice. We call it *sabzi-polo-mahi.* Nowruz might be my favorite holiday. I guess I like new years and new beginnings."

Cabe nodded thoughtfully. "I do, too. That's actually sort of why I'm here. I was hoping *we* could start fresh." I smiled, and he let out a breath. "Phew. I'm hoping that means I got something right today?" I nodded, my mouth watering at the delicious floral and honeyed smell drifting from the pastry box. "So can you hang out for a while?" Cabe asked. "Ben could drive us someplace."

I hesitated. "Can I ask why you want to?"

He fidgeted with his jacket zipper. "I'll be out of school doing nonstop filming with Sonora, so I might not see you for the next couple of days."

I blushed. Was he trying to say he'd miss me? My heart and mind began arguing over what to do, and for better or worse, my heart won out. "Okay. I can't handle going home yet anyway. We could head over to Holey Donuts. It's another great donut place in the West Village."

He laughed. "Won't you be doughed-out after the *bamieh*?"

"Never."

"Okay."

After we both texted our parents to let them know what we'd be doing, I gave Ben directions, and the limo started moving through the snowy streets.

"So, tell me," Cabe said.

"What do you mean?" I asked.

"I mean, tell me why you don't want to go home. I could tell the second I saw you this morning at school that something was wrong, so spill it."

"You could?" He nodded, looking at me with such intensity that I wondered what else he noticed about me.

"Okay," I said and started talking, about Mina and my parents, and about my blow-up with them this morning. As I talked, Cabe and I shared the bite-sized *bamieh*, careful not to spill too many crumbs in the backseat. Once I got started, the words came easier and easier. Cabe was a great listener, and I felt myself lightening as I vented.

"I guess I just exploded," I finished.

"Maybe you needed to," Cabe said. He watched me as I popped another *bamieh* into my mouth. "Seems like you had a lot to say. So you said it."

I laughed. "That's not what I do. I keep the peace."

"But if there are problems, how peaceful can things really be?" Cabe asked, and then he paused. "When Kiri and I were working on our history project, she told me she worries about you. She thinks you don't speak up enough, and that if she's not around, people might take advantage of that and . . ."

"What?" I asked, frustration simmering under my skin. "Walk all over me?" That was ironic, because lately, I'd felt like Kiri was doing that to me. "I can hold my own," I blurted out, more fiercely than I intended.

Cabe's eyes widened in surprise, but then he grinned. "That's exactly what I said. I think you're braver than you realize. I mean, you've never acted before in your life—but you're trying."

"And never will again," I said with a short laugh.

"But it takes guts to do something way out of your comfort zone like that."

"Thanks. I surprised myself a little, too, just by surviving it."

Ben dropped us off in front of Washington Square Park. Cabe and I paused to watch the snow swirling around the great white arch at its entrance. A group of kids was busy making snowmen on the park benches.

"It's nice like this," Cabe said as we started walking. "The city. The last few weeks, it's been growing on me. And I keep thinking about the Off-Broadway theaters. How cool it would be to get back to more stage acting. Maybe plays at smaller venues, with challenging roles." Enthusiasm lit up his face. "I'm going to talk to my manager about that."

"So does that mean you're moving here then?" My pulse fluttered.

"I still don't know. There's a lot I like about being here. It feels more authentic than Hollywood, and I'm even getting used to winter." He tucked his hands deeper into his jacket. "I thought I'd have another, even better reason to stay, but . . ." He buried his face into his collar. "I'm not sure."

"What was the reason?" I asked, suddenly feeling that he'd been on the verge of saying something important. But then Cabe announced loudly, "We're here!"

"Oh. Yeah."

He rushed into Holey Donuts ahead of me, and if I hadn't known better, I would've sworn he was nervous. He fidgeted and avoided my eyes while we ordered and ate our donuts. When I asked him how he liked his strawberry sprinkle donut, he barely said two words about it. By the time we made the walk back to my apartment, I was replaying everything I'd said over the last hour, wondering how I'd made him this out of sorts. But then, as we stepped onto my block, he grabbed my hand.

"Sheyda, wait." He blew out a puff of air from his cheeks. "Wow, it's crazy how nervous I am right now," he mumbled, almost to himself. "What I said about that kiss—our kiss—to Kiri. About it being fake. That wasn't true. It was great. More than great! I panicked, or maybe I just wanted to tell you in private. The thing is . . ." He swallowed. "*I* was the one who asked Simeon to hire you for *Donut Go Breaking My Heart.*"

I stared at him as my insides puddled, trying to make sense of his words over my deafening heartbeat. "What?" I managed. "Why?"

"I wanted to get to know you better." His eyes were hopeful. "From the first time I saw you, I wanted to be around you all the time. Even when you were mad about me being so rude to you." He smiled so sweetly that I had to resist the urge to hug him right there in the middle of the sidewalk. "I can't explain it, but there it is. I *finally* said it. And . . . I wanted to ask you if you'd go with me to the premiere of *Very Valentine.*"

A rush of joy swept over me. I'd been telling myself for so long that it was impossible, but here Cabe was, saying he liked me! I hadn't even realized how much I wanted it to be true until it was. He saw the happiness on my face and stepped closer. "Is that a yes?" he asked softly, and for one second I was sure we'd kiss again. And then I remembered—

Kiri. What would it do to Kiri if I went to the premiere with Cabe? Worse, what would she do when she found out I liked him, after I'd denied it? Yes, I was annoyed with Kiri right now. But if I said yes to being his date, it would be like stabbing her in the back.

Reality brought my bliss to a screeching halt. "Cabe, wait." My voice hitched. "I can't."

The hope in his face extinguished, replaced with confusion. "So, you won't be my date, or you don't like me?"

My throat tightened, every fiber in me wanting to shout out the truth. Instead, I forced out a gut-wrenching, "I do like you . . . just not that way. I'm . . . so sorry." My lower lip was quivering now. I was going to cry, but I couldn't do it in front of him. "I have to go—"

It was painful to look at him. His face was glowing red with hurt and embarrassment. "Wow," he said quietly. "I guess I sounded pretty lame just now, huh?"

"No!" I blurted. "Everything you said was so, so sweet. It's not you. It's me." Oh no. My eyes were filling. "I—I'll never forget it." The tears were going to spill. I turned away, hurrying down the sidewalk. "About the premiere," I called over my shoulder. "You should ask Kiri!"

"Kiri?" His voice was puzzled. "Sheyda, wait!"

I didn't look back, but it didn't matter. For the rest of the night, I had a picture in my head of him, standing alone on the sidewalk in the snow, watching me leave.

Chapter Ten

I yawned over my bowl of cereal, barely able to keep my eyes open. It was Friday: D-day for my camp application. Jillian had messengered her reference letter to our apartment last night, and I'd finished my model around two in the morning, working at the kitchen table while my parents and Mina slept. Just in the nick of time, too, because Ms. Feld was expecting to see it first thing this morning.

"Are you girls okay to get ready on your own this morning?"

my father asked as he set his coffee in the sink and grabbed his briefcase. "I've got to be in court by eight."

"Me, too," Mom added, giving us both pecks on the cheeks.

My cereal stuck in my throat. So they'd forgotten about the promise they'd made weeks ago to drive me to school when my model was ready for Ms. Feld's approval. They'd probably forgotten that my application due date was today, too. I thought about reminding them; carrying the model to school through slushy streets wasn't the best idea. But then what? It wasn't like they could be late for court. I'd get the model to school and then text Mom later to remind her that she needed to drive me down to NYU to turn it in by 5 p.m.

"We'll be fine." I sighed. "Have a good day."

I glanced at Mina, who gave my parents a silent nod. She'd barely spoken to me since our argument on Monday, and Mom, aside from a brief "let's talk about what happened later" comment, hadn't brought up my meltdown, either. She was always distracted when she was in the middle of litigation.

As soon as the door clicked shut on my parents, Mina was out of her chair and gathering her stuff from our room. I wouldn't have even noticed the duffel bag slung over her arm, except that it got stuck in the door handle when she went to leave. The zipper was partially open, and I caught a glimpse of Mina's gray skull-and-crossbones ski pants inside. Huh? She never took anything to school but her messenger bag.

"What's the duffel for?" I asked.

"Lending Rehann clothes for her ski weekend" was all she said, and then she was gone.

I sat back in the chair, listening to the silence of the apartment. Silence was the way most of this week had gone. I hadn't talked to Cabe since Monday. He'd been out of school all week filming with Sonora Grace at Doughlicious. The texts and calls from him before had stopped completely. He'd taken my advice and asked Kiri to be his date for the *Very Valentine* premiere. I'd gotten a text from her only an hour after I'd left Cabe in the snow. I tried not to be hurt by that, remembering that he was hurt, too. But it didn't help that Kiri had taken to texting me dozens of times a day just to gush over it. It only made my heart ache more.

Since then, I'd only spoken to Kiri when I had to. On our walks to school, I'd feigned interest in a game on my phone, and I'd spent lunches in the library, finishing my essay for my camp application. It was a legit excuse, but I knew the real reason I was skipping lunch was to avoid Kiri. Phoebe seemed to suspect it, too, because she'd shown up in the library once, pulling up a chair and saying bluntly, "Spill it."

When I didn't after a few minutes, she'd nodded and stood up. "Sheyda, you have to tell her. It's no crime that you like Cabe, and I'm guessing your 'like' is realer than hers, not that I'm judging. But it's not fair that she doesn't even know how you feel."

I'd kept thinking, *How can Phoebe see the truth and Kiri can't? I shouldn't have to spell it out for Kiri.*

I finished breakfast and carefully slipped a trash bag over my model to protect it. Then I headed for school. I had to be there early to meet with Ms. Feld, so thankfully I wouldn't see Kiri until later. But even the relief I felt in finally finishing the model couldn't overcome the sadness of having to celebrate its completion alone.

Ten minutes later, I nearly dropped the model in surprise when I saw Kiri sitting on the school steps.

"There you are!" She smiled. "Today's the big day! Are you nervous? I'm so glad you finally showed. My toes are freezing!" She held up a Doughlicious bag. "I brought your favorite to celebrate. A Cheesecake Crumble, still warm."

"Thanks. You . . . you remembered today was my deadline?" I asked.

She rolled her eyes. "I'm your best friend. Of course I remembered." She peered over my shoulder. "But wait, where's the car? I thought your parents were going to drive you today."

I shrugged. "I decided to walk," I said simply.

"You should've texted me, silly. Mom would've come to get you."

"It doesn't matter," I mumbled. "I'm here now." I suddenly realized her cane and bandage were MIA. "How's the ankle?"

"So much better!" she said. "Like it never happened."

"Mmmmm," I said, and thought, *It probably never did.*

She tilted her head. "Hey. Is everything okay? 'Cause you've been acting strange all week. It's like you've been avoiding me."

My heart bolted. "It's fine," I told her. "I'm fine." I focused my eyes on the model. "I better get this inside."

Together, we eased the model through the school doors and hallways to the theater. Ms. Feld was waiting in her office, her eyes bright, her multi-ringed hands clasped in anticipation.

My own hands shook as I slid the garbage bag from the model, but Kiri's were steady, holding the foam board below. Ms. Feld and Kiri stared down at the model.

"Sheyda," Kiri breathed. "It's fantastic."

I set the model on Ms. Feld's desk, and Kiri and Ms. Feld bent over it, examining the details. "See, the entire set sits on a rotating base," I explained. "One side is the world of Romeo and Juliet's past. The other side is their future. When it's time for a transition from past to future, the stagehands rotate the set like one big revolving secret door."

On the future side, there was a backdrop of sleek furniture, the suspended spiral staircase, and a city sky speckled with droids and hovercrafts. The past side had the balconies and old-fashioned homes of fourteenth-century Verona, Italy.

Ms. Feld bowed her head toward me. "Brava! I won't jinx it by saying it's a shoo-in, but I predict an acceptance *and* a scholarship."

I blushed with pride and relief. "Thanks. I just hate that I can't take the model to NYU right now. How am I going to keep it safe all day at school?"

Ms. Feld waved a hand over the model. "Leave it to me. The model will be fine in my office. I'll lock the door if I step out."

"Okay," I said.

The bell rang, and Kiri and I grabbed our bags to go find Phoebe and Val. But I kept glancing at the model, not wanting to leave it, until Ms. Feld laughed and shooed me away.

Even with Kiri's encouragement, I left the theater reluctantly, knowing I'd still worry until my model was safe at the NYU admissions office. It was going to be a long day.

*　　*　　*

"Sheyda Nazari."

I jerked my head off my desk at the sound of my name, my pulse racing. I'd been trying to pay attention to Mrs. Milano's history lecture, but it was seventh period, the room was as warm as a toaster, and I was exhausted. Now, I tried to look as alert as possible.

"You've been asked to report to the office."

"Oh." I gulped, scrambling to grab my books as I glanced at the clock. There were only ten minutes left of school. This couldn't be good. I hurried out of the room and down the hallway, thinking about my math test, with its bright red *D*, sitting heavily in my schoolbag. That had to be what this was about. Mr. Quinten had handed the test back to me in first period with a disappointed shake of his head, and now he'd probably called Mom and Dad to tell them the news. As if worrying about how my model was doing in Ms. Feld's office wasn't bad enough, now I had an awful grade to tell my parents about tonight, too. Stress? I had some.

When I stepped into the office, though, Mr. Quinten wasn't anywhere in sight. Instead, the school secretary held out the office phone to me.

"Your mom's on the line," she said.

I frowned. I'd texted Mom before the start of seventh period to ask her to drive me down to NYU, and she'd said she'd meet me outside the school. I always turned off my cell during class, but I couldn't remember Mom ever calling the school before.

"Mom?" I said into the phone, dread stealing over me.

"Sheyda." Mom's voice was tight. "Mina's school just called. She didn't show up for last period this afternoon, and her cell's going straight to voicemail. I tried using the cell tracker app to find her, but she must've turned hers off because it's not working. We have no idea where she is. Do you?"

"No," I said. "She's probably hanging out with Rehann or—" I froze, my mind suddenly flashing back to the duffel bag Mina had been toting this morning. "Wait a sec, isn't this the weekend of Rehann's family ski trip?"

"What? I—I suppose so, but you don't think Mina would—"

"Mom. Mina had her duffel bag when she left this morning and her ski pants were in it."

There was a gasp on the other end of the line, and then, "I have to go. Right now. I'm heading to Rehann's house. You go straight to Doughlicious after school. Wait there until I call."

"But, Mom. What about—"

My application, I thought as the line went dead. The final bell rang at the same moment. The anger started in my chest and flashed through my body like lightning, quick and fierce. Anger at Mina, at my parents. Why did Mina have to do this, today of all days?

I rushed out of the office, heading for the theater to get my model. I texted Kiri as I walked, asking her if she could call her mom to ask about driving me. The fact that my model was still in perfect shape when I reached Ms. Feld's office seemed like the only plus of the day so far. I responded faintly to Ms. Feld's wish of luck as I carefully maneuvered the model through her office door. Kids from the glee club were starting to crowd the wings of the stage for their after-school practice, and I had to duck and weave around them to keep them from knocking into the model. Val was there, too, and when she saw me with the model, she made a protective circle with her arms around me, trying to ward off anyone getting too close.

"Stay back. Precious cargo coming through," Val warned in a voice about as scary as a mouse's. Still, I appreciated her sweet effort.

I was holding my breath, praying I'd make it out of the school with the model intact when Kiri came rushing toward us, her face pale and frantic.

"Guys! I lost my lucky necklace," she cried, groping at the empty space where it usually sat along her collarbone. "I had it on this morning, like always, and I didn't even realize it was missing until a few minutes ago." Her lip trembled. "Sheyda, you gave it to me. I *have* to find it."

"Okay, okay," I said, setting my model down on the edge of the stage to help her look for it. Val put her arm around Kiri, offering comfort, but Kiri looked so beside herself. "You said you had it this morning," I thought out loud. "We walked into the theater with the model." I headed for the stairs leading to the theater seats. "Let's check the aisles."

I bent over, searching under seats and along the edge of the dark red carpet. Val and Kiri did the same. It took a few minutes, but I finally spotted it, dangling from an armrest halfway up the aisle. "Found it!" I cried.

Kiri's face lit up just as I heard the ominous crunch from the direction of the stage.

"Oops." Terry, one of the glee club's lead singers, stared down mournfully at my model, then up at me. "I didn't see it there. I'm sorry."

I dropped Kiri's necklace into her palm and ran to the stage. My model was in pieces, the suspended staircase crushed, the backdrops warped. I picked it up, shaking my head in disbelief and panic.

"No," I whispered. "No, no, no, no, no!"

"Oh, Sheyda." Val was already tearing up.

Kiri peered at the model, her hand cupped over her mouth. "Let me take a look. Maybe we can fix it together—"

I spun on her, the dam breaking. "I can't fix that!" I cried. "It's ruined. Ruined! And—and it's your fault!"

"Guys," Val started, her expression pleading for peace, "come on—"

"My fault?" Kiri stared at me, stunned.

"Yes! You and that stupid necklace, and just . . . everything!" My eyes welled. "You faked that sprained ankle, didn't you? So that you could stage that kiss with Cabe?"

Kiri frowned. "Are you saying that I lied? I don't lie—"

I snorted. "No, you just act your way into getting whatever you want. And I'm sick of you speaking *for* me all the time. I have my own thoughts and feelings, only I never get the chance to say them before you do. And—and you're wrong most of the time about them anyway!"

She balked. "What are you talking about? I look out for you, and you hate me for it?" Her voice was quavering, too. "What about me? How do you think I feel whenever Mom brags about you to customers? Or whenever she says stuff like, 'You should be more like Sheyda.'" She bit her lip, all traces of her usual confidence and composure gone. "She should have had you as a daughter instead of me."

I stared at her in shock. I'd never realized she'd felt like that before. But then my anger returned in a flash. No. I wasn't going to let her make this all about her. Not anymore. I glared at her, tears coursing down my cheeks. "You don't even like Cabe, do you? Not really. You only want to go to the premiere with him because you think it'll get you an acting job."

"I like him!" Kiri protested, looking uncomfortable. "Maybe not '*like* like,' but I could. I don't have to know how I feel about him right now."

"You *should* know! I do!" I started pacing, fists clenched. "It's wrong, what you're doing! You can't mess with his head like that. He'll end up getting hurt, and I'm not going to just sit back and let that happen . . ." I wiped at my eyes, but when I glanced up at Kiri, I saw she was crying, too. Then, realization dawned on her face.

"Oh, Sheyda," she whispered, her eyes widening. "Why didn't you tell me you liked him?" She glanced at Val. "Did you know about this?"

Val bit her lip. "Um, I kind of suspected . . ."

Kiri shook her head at me. "I asked you before, and you said—"

"I know what I said, but I lied, okay? I knew you were interested in him, and I didn't want to get in the way." My voice shook. "I should've said something. I should say a lot more than I do. I know that now. But . . ." I heaved a sigh. "It's too late. And my model." I choked back a sob. "My model's ruined."

I grabbed my bag and ran up the aisle.

"Sheyda!" Val called after me.

"What about your model?" Kiri cried. "Sheyda! Wait! Don't go! Donuts!"

I nearly stopped when I heard our code word.

"*Donuts!*" Kiri called out again, more desperately this time.

But I was done doing what she told me to. Everything I'd been working toward was lying in a crumpled pile back there on the stage, and all I wanted to do was go home and cry until I didn't have a single teardrop left.

Chapter Eleven

The buzzing came through my dream loudly, like a pesky bumblebee. My eyes were swollen from crying. I didn't want to open them, but the buzzing kept going. I pulled myself off the bed to peek at the clock.

Five p.m. I didn't remember falling asleep, only stumbling into the apartment and locking myself in my bedroom before crumpling onto the bed for a good, long cry. I was sure Mrs. Seng had called my parents by now to tell them that I'd never shown up at Doughlicious, but I'd set my cell to "silent" and hadn't checked it since I'd left school. For all I knew my parents could be driving up to Vermont to bring Mina home.

The buzzer sounded again. "Go away," I mumbled. But when it didn't stop, I reluctantly yanked open my bedroom door and went to the intercom in the hallway.

I pushed the button to listen, then waited. "Sheyda," Cabe's voice crackled through the speaker. "I know you're in there. Please. Open the door."

My heart bounced at his voice, but I instantly scolded it. That was all done now. Cabe and Kiri were going to be a couple. I'd have to accept it. So would my disobedient heart. "Cabe, this . . . isn't a good time," I muttered into the intercom. "I thought you were working today."

"I was, but Kiri called me. She told me what happened with your model, and . . ." I couldn't tell if he paused or if the speaker cut out momentarily. *Oh no,* I panicked. *Please tell me she didn't tell him everything.* "She feels terrible. She asked me to check on you."

"If she feels so terrible, then why isn't she here?" I sounded mean now, but I didn't care. "I don't need anyone checking on me. I'm fine."

"You don't sound fine," Cabe retorted. "Look, can you buzz me in? I'm carrying something fragile and I really don't want anything else to happen to it."

What was he talking about? I went to the family room window and peered down. Cabe was standing on the stoop cradling a large garbage bag in his arms. A lump formed in my throat. That couldn't be what I thought it was . . . could it? I hit the button that unlocked the front door of the building, then listened to Cabe's steps on the hall stairs, my heart pounding in time with his footfalls.

When I opened the front door, Cabe held the garbage bag out toward me. "I brought you something." His eyes roamed my face, taking in my puffy eyes and red nose and cheeks. "And I think it's my turn to say I'm sorry."

"For what?" I took the garbage bag, feeling the familiar edges of my model resting inside. A fresh wave of pain broke over me. I didn't want to look at it in pieces. I stepped toward the trash can, prepared to dump the entire thing inside, unseen.

"Wait!" He grabbed my arm. "What are you doing?"

"Tossing it," I said. "It's completely destroyed . . ."

"No. Here." He slid the garbage bag off the model, and I gasped, staring. Someone had repaired it, painstakingly gluing the pieces of the staircase back in place, smoothing out the crumpled backdrop. If I looked closely, I could still see slight warps in the scenery, and a few crooked stairs. But for the most part, it didn't look too bad. It almost looked . . . submittable. "I met Kiri at the school after she called me. We tried to fix the model. Ms. Feld had some glue. Phoebe and Val helped, too. But we're not sure we got everything right." He offered up a small smile. "It needs your touch."

I set it on the kitchen table, then sank into a chair beside it, speechless. Cabe slid into the chair beside me.

"Thank you," I whispered. "I can't believe you fixed it. And Kiri." My brow furrowed. "But I already missed the deadline. The application was due at five." I glanced at the clock. "It's half past now. It's a lost cause."

"Don't worry about that," Cabe said. "I called NYU. The

administrative assistant in the camp admissions office said she'd still accept your application if you turned it in by seven tonight. She'll make an exception for me—er, you."

I narrowed my eyes. "Wait a sec. She fell for the Cabe Sadler charm, didn't she?"

"I might've promised her an autographed poster. I can't help it if she's a fan." He grinned sheepishly. "There are times when being famous has its perks." I let myself laugh a little at that. "So . . ." he added quietly. "Do you want to hear what I'm sorry for?" His blue eyes searched mine. I nodded as my heart began to thunder. "I'm sorry I didn't get what was going on," he said quietly. "That I didn't understand why you said no when I asked you to go with me to the premiere."

"What did Kiri tell you? That I . . . ?" *Like you,* I thought, but I couldn't get the words out. I shook my head. "Don't feel sorry for me—"

"Is that what you think this is?" he blurted, then grabbed my hand. "It's not about that at all. The thing is that me and Kiri . . ." He blew out a breath. "I asked her to go to the premiere with me because *you* wouldn't. You told me to ask her, remember? I really wanted to go with you, but then you didn't want to, and my manager kept telling me I had to have a date. I didn't want to ask anybody else, but Kiri's nice, even if she did play up the ankle thing."

I stared at him. "Y-you realized that?"

He laughed. "Sprained ankles swell. They even bruise sometimes. I got one filming *Very Valentine*. I saw Kiri's ankle before it was bandaged. It was fine."

"But—but you gave her that cane, and—"

"That was Simeon and Jillian's idea. They wanted to see how long she could stay 'in character.' They watched her whole walking-wounded performance. It was like an audition. And they were impressed. They want her for a role in a rom-com they're planning."

"Wow." My mind spun, then I frowned. "You could've told me you knew she was faking."

"Simeon didn't want anyone tipping off Kiri until they were sure they wanted to hire her. Besides, I wasn't sure *you* knew she was faking. And she's your best friend, so I wasn't about to call her on it. You two are pretty inseparable."

My face fell. "Not anymore."

Cabe paused. "Kiri puts on a good act, but I think she's more unsure of herself than she seems. Out of the two of you, you're the stronger one."

"What?" I snorted.

He motioned to my model. "You're not using tricks to go after what you want. You don't name-drop or kiss up. You just do your thing, no matter what." He smiled. "You probably don't realize it, but your bravery's made me braver, too."

"Yeah, right."

"It's true," he said. "I wouldn't have given New York a fair shot without you. You helped me see it through your eyes, not the way a tourist would. And I *am* going back to stage acting. My manager's psyched and already lined up some auditions for me. I feel more excited about acting than I've felt in a long time, and it's thanks to you. And New York. I actually can't wait to experience more of it now." He grinned. "I still have to take the subway and bike the loop in Central Park . . . so many cool things."

It was like a trapdoor had opened on the stage of my life, and my heart had just fallen through, into Cabe's hands. "So . . . does that mean you're staying in New York?"

Cabe nodded. "We just decided for sure last night. You're the first person I've told. I have to fly to France right after Valentine's Day to finish filming *Donut*." He rolled his eyes. "It's Prince Dalton's 'kingdom.'" He put finger quotes around "kingdom." "But when the filming wraps up, my dad will fly back to California to rent out our house in LA. He's already found an apartment here."

"That's great!" I said, my voice swooping high.

He glanced at me hopefully. "Is it?"

The way he said it was like he was asking about more than just his move. I blushed. I'd promised myself I was done keeping everything bottled up inside. Now it was time to be true to my word. "Kiri might've told you already, but . . . I need you to hear it from me." Omigod, I was really going to do this. "I wasn't honest with you when you asked me to go to the premiere. I wanted to go with you. Really badly. But I knew Kiri was hoping you'd ask her, and I didn't want to hurt her feelings." I risked a peek at his face and saw his eyes lighting up. "The thing is . . . I like you. A lot."

A smile stretched across his face, and he squeezed my hand. "Me too." He brushed a hand across my cheek. "Do you know what my best reason for wanting to stay in New York is?" I shook my head. "You."

Relief and a giddy happiness filled me as Cabe folded me into a hug. But that was until he asked, "So does this mean you'll go with me to the premiere?"

I hesitated. "I can't promise that yet. I think I have to talk to Kiri first." In fact, Kiri wasn't the only one I needed to talk to. My parents and Mina flickered through my mind.

He nodded slowly. "I figured that. But you'll for sure let me know?"

I smiled. "Definitely."

He held my gaze so long, then said, "I really want to kiss you right now, but . . ."

I knew he was thinking about Kiri and whether she'd be okay when I told her about the two of us. I was thinking about her, too, but there was something else. "My model!" I cried. I'd suddenly snapped out of my Cabe delirium long enough to remember. I leaned over it, scrutinizing every inch of the miniature stage. "I think I should reinforce the rotation device, and maybe replace a couple steps on the staircase completely . . ."

Cabe laughed, then sobered as an insistent honking sounded from outside. "Uh-oh," he said, paling. "She's really peeved now."

"Who? Kiri?" I asked. The honking turned into a long blare. Whoever she was, she was laying on the horn.

Cabe clenched his eyes shut, shaking his head. "It's Sonora. We were in the middle of a shoot in Tompkins Square Park when I got Kiri's phone call. Since I was filming, Ben took the afternoon off, so I had to beg Sonora to use her limo to get to school and Doughlicious and then—"

There was a pounding on the door. "Here," Cabe finished, giving me a helpless smile.

I headed for the door as Cabe added, "Just . . . don't mention donuts."

"What? Why?" But then I opened the door and understood. An impossibly tall, slender, and of course beautiful girl blew into the kitchen, covered head to toe in powdered sugar.

"Cabe Sadler!" she fumed. "Who leaves a box of donuts on a back dash? This is a silk coat! Ruined!"

"I'll pay for the dry cleaning," Cabe said, his tone barely masking a stifled laugh. He glanced at me, his eyes playful. "Kiri sent us over with brain food for you, but there was a little accident—"

"Little!" Sonora shook powdered sugar from her auburn curls. "Just how much longer is this plebeian problem going to take?" She eyed my model. "We slugged through rush hour traffic for *that*?"

Whoa, I thought. This girl was every bit the wicked witch they'd said she was.

"Sheyda just has to make a few tweaks," Cabe started. "Then we'd so appreciate a ride to NYU to drop it off."

"Whatev. But can you make it quick? I have plans tonight."

I smiled sweetly. Nothing—not even Sonora Grace—could dampen my spirits now. In a moment of brashness, I stuck a container of wood glue into her palm. "Why don't you help? That will make it go faster."

She stared at me, then at Cabe. "Is this girl for real?"

"Absolutely," Cabe answered.

Sonora mumbled a string of indecipherable words. Then, "Fine. Show me what to glue."

I pointed to a spot, and as she started gluing, I whispered to Cabe, "That donut spill wasn't an accident, was it?"

He grinned. "Not a chance. But after working with her today, it had to be done. You have *no* idea."

I slapped his arm teasingly, then squeezed his hand, whispering, "Thank you."

Leaving them in the kitchen, I raced to my bedroom to get the rest of my design supplies. I had one hour, at best, and a lot of work to do between now and then.

* * *

When I walked back into my apartment two hours later, Mom and Dad leapt up from the kitchen table, both shouting at once. "Sheyda, where have you been?" "We've been calling your cell phone for hours!" "Why didn't you answer your phone?" "We were worried sick!"

"I had to go down to NYU to turn in my application," I said calmly. As that sunk in, their expressions turned from rage to guilt.

"Oh, Sheyda." Mom slapped a hand over her mouth. "I'm so sorry. When Mina went missing, I got so worried, and I—I completely forgot."

I nodded. Part of me wanted to say that it was okay. Instinct told me that I should make them feel better about it, but maybe this time, I needed them to listen to me first. "I know you did," I said, coming in to sit down at the table. "It's been weeks since you even asked me how it was going. You didn't even get to see it before I turned it in."

"Well, I'm sure it was perfect," Dad said quickly. "Your work always is."

I shook my head. "But that's just it, Dad. It wasn't. There was an accident at school today, and the model got smashed." Mom's eyes widened with concern. "It ended up being okay," I pushed on. "We fixed it. But . . . it's not going to be perfect. And, I'm not, either."

"Sheyda." Mom reached for my hand. "We know that—"

"I'm not sure you do." I took a deep breath as my pulse rattled. I needed to get it all out now, everything I wanted to say while I was still feeling brave enough. "I act like I can handle everything with school and stuff. I try so hard to do it all right so that everyone will stay happy. You both worry about Mina so much—" My breath caught when I realized I hadn't even asked about her yet. "Where *is* Mina?"

Mom waved her hand. "In her room. Grounded for life . . . We'll talk about Mina later. This is about *you*."

My lips trembled. I almost wanted to cry, hearing those words. "You both worry about Mina so much," I began again, "and I thought that if I kept doing well, and doing everything like I should, then you'd have one less thing to worry about."

"But you're not a thing," Dad said quietly. "You're our daughter. We worry about you, too."

My eyebrows shot up in surprise. "You . . . you do?"

Mom gave a tired laugh. "Of course we do! You're so quiet, and we worry that you put too much pressure on yourself. But lately . . ." She sighed. "We *have* been preoccupied with Mina, I suppose. She's always seemed to need more from us than you have."

"I know you think that," I said. "It's like it's a given that she's always wild and I'm always good. But maybe neither one of us is always one way or the other. We just . . . are. Me and her. And it's okay if we change."

"Oh no." Mom put her head in her hands. "You're going to rebel, too."

I laughed. "Not right now. Maybe not ever, but I don't know. And the thing is, I need you to worry about me, too. Not all the time. But maybe sometimes?" My voice broke on my last word, and then Mom and Dad were both out of their chairs and wrapping their arms around me.

"We were so stupid," Dad said. "We just assumed you were doing fine. You never said anything—"

"I know." I looked at both of them, smiling. "That's going to change. I want to be able to tell you when I'm feeling overwhelmed. I don't want to feel jealous of Mina for getting so much attention . . ."

"Wait a sec." I heard Mina's voice, and I glanced up to see her leaning against the hallway wall. "*You're* jealous of me?"

She sounded so shocked that I giggled. "Sure. A little. I mean, it took serious guts to try to sneak off on that ski trip."

"Sheyda!" blurted Mom.

"Thanks." Mina laughed. "At least I tried."

Dad shot Mina a stern look. "And you'll never try anything like it again, if you know what's good for you."

Mina held up her hands. "Believe me, I know. I'm going to be paying for it for forever." She wrinkled her nose, but she didn't look nearly as upset about it as I'd expected.

"Wait a sec," I said. "Why don't you look madder?"

Mina shrugged. "Oh, I'm mad, believe me. But not knowing where you were freaked me out, too. You never go rogue, and I felt like maybe it might be my fault, for losing it with you earlier this week."

"*And* giving me the silent treatment when I didn't even tell on you," I added, shooting her a look.

"Yeah," she said grudgingly. "That too, I guess. It made me think that there are more important things in life than ski trips." She gave me a grudging smile. "Like sisters." She hurriedly walked over to hug me. "I—I'm glad you're home safe."

"Thanks," I said as she pulled away and glanced at our parents.

"Maybe you'll consider shortening my sentence for exhibiting good sisterly behavior?" she asked them.

"Back to your room," Dad growled.

"Fine. I'm going. I'm going." Mina rolled her eyes at me, and then we both grinned. She still had a lot of things to work on with my parents, and I guessed that she probably wouldn't be seeing much of Rehann and Josh for a while. But maybe if she was grounded for that long, she and I would get to spend a little more time together.

It was something to hope for, at least.

Once Mina was gone, Mom bent over me, kissing my forehead in a way she hadn't done since I was a lot smaller. "We love you," she whispered. "You never have to be perfect for our sakes or anyone else's."

"Good," I said, hugging her back as my heart filled with warmth, "because, um, I just got a test back in math today, and I got a horrible grade."

Dad straightened. "Well, then, we better talk about it. Don't you think?"

His words made me feel even more relieved. I nodded. "That's a good idea."

Chapter Twelve

"Do you want me to go in with you, *aziz?*" Mom asked in the predawn stillness of the street. Even though it was Saturday, the only day of the week she and Dad usually slept in, she'd gotten up early to come with me. We hadn't talked much on the walk, but just having her beside me, her arm occasionally brushing against mine, felt like the start of something new and cozy between us. I couldn't remember the last time Mom had taken a break from her busy schedule to just *be* with me, and even though

I was so nervous about what I was about to do, having her beside me made me feel braver.

Now, I glanced at the front window of Doughlicious, empty and waiting for the first fresh batches of donuts to fill its display shelves. Kiri, I knew, would be in the kitchen with Mrs. Seng, baking. "Thanks, Mom, but I should do this alone." I gave her a tremulous smile.

She squeezed my hand. "I'll be waiting if you need me."

That made all the difference. I took a deep breath, then pushed open the door. The second I did, the chimes sounded and Mrs. Seng came out of the kitchen in her apron.

"Can I help—" When she saw me, she nodded in understanding. "Kiri's in the kitchen."

"Thanks."

Kiri was just pulling a steaming tray of Cherry Cobbler donuts from the oven when I walked in. They smelled heavenly. Her eyes caught mine, her expression a mixture of sadness and uncertainty. Wow. Did I look as nervous as she did?

"Can I help?" I asked softly.

She shrugged. "You know where your apron is."

I slipped it over my head, thinking about how many hundreds of times we'd done this together through the years, how naturally we took up our stations at the counter and oven, working side by side. She set the tray on the counter in front of me, and I grabbed the sifter. Holding it over the donuts, I tapped the side and watched as powdered sugar fluttered down on the donuts like snow.

We worked for a few minutes in silence, and while I wasn't sure how Kiri would react once I started talking, I took it as a good sign that she wasn't throwing me out *or* rambling on and on. She seemed to be waiting for me to go first, which was something new, for both of us.

"Thank you," I finally said, "for fixing my model."

She paused mid-step, another hot tray in her mitted hands. "Did they still let you turn it in?"

I nodded, and her face broke into a relieved smile. "Oh, I'm so glad! I was worried they wouldn't accept it late . . ."

"I figured you already knew. That you'd checked in with Cabe."

She shook her head. "I didn't. I thought it might be better for you and Cabe to work things out without me getting involved. But—oh my gosh!—was it hard to hold back!" I couldn't help but laugh. "Please tell me, because I can't stand it anymore. Are you going to the premiere with him?"

I took the next tray from her and began sprinkling. "I don't know." I swallowed. "I told him I needed to talk to you first." I turned to face her fully. "The thing is, I can't go to the premiere with him if it's going to hurt you. I like him. You know that now. But I don't want a boy to mess with our friendship. Because I love you too much."

Kiri rushed forward, throwing her arms around me so hard that we both nearly toppled onto the floor. I caught myself against the counter just in time.

"I love you, too!" she cried. "And you were totally right. I didn't want to admit it, because I knew it wasn't one of my better moments as a person, but . . ." She whooshed out a breath. "I *did* fake my sprained ankle. It was horrible, I know, but all I could think about was that if I could stage a kiss with Cabe in front of the press, I'd finally get my big break."

I shook my head. "Kiri, you're super talented. You don't need to rely on someone else's success for your own."

She glanced at me doubtfully. "Thanks, but I don't always feel that way, and I get so tired of Mom reminding me that if acting doesn't work out, I'll always have donuts."

I giggled. "That should be a line in *Donut Go Breaking My Heart*."

Kiri snarfed out a giggle, too. "It does sound like a cheesy movie line, doesn't it?" She sighed. "I shouldn't have used Cabe the way I did, like he was some kind of fast track to fame."

"The only fast track you need is your own," I said. "Jillian and Simeon have been watching you. I don't know for sure, but I have it on good authority that they might be asking you to play some parts in movies down the road."

Kiri's shriek of excitement made my ears ring. "Omigod, omigod, omigod. Mom, did you hear that?"

"Not a word" came Mrs. Seng's voice from the other side of the door.

"A legit movie actress!" Kiri hollered.

"Humph," said the door.

Kiri grinned at me, then grew serious. "I wish you'd told me how you felt about Cabe a long time ago." She tilted her head at me. "You can be tough to figure out, and you can't always expect people to read your mind. You've got to spit it out or else nobody will know what you're feeling."

I nodded. "But sometimes you're not that easy to talk to. You get a little wrapped up in . . . in . . ."

"Myself?" Kiri rolled her eyes. "No newsflash there. Mom's been reminding me since birth. But hey, you're my BFF and that's part of your job. To keep me in check. If you can't do it, who can?"

"If that's what you want," I said hesitantly.

"I do!" She looked at me, waiting to see if I'd take her up on it.

"Here goes." I held up a hand and ticked off one finger at a time. "Talk to your mom about the way she is with your acting.

Tell her it hurts your feelings when she compares me to you." Kiri nodded, and I hurried on. "And quit telling everyone how shy I am. I might be shy, but I don't need you to do all the talking for me anymore. I'm planning on doing a lot more on my own."

Kiri's eyes filled with tears—real ones. No acting. "You're so right, Sheyda," she said softly. "I'm sorry about everything."

"Me too."

She reached for a napkin to dab her eyes but ended up getting powdered sugar on her face. Then we were both laughing and flicking puffs of powdered sugar at each other. We only quit when Mrs. Seng stuck her head around the door. She glared, but there was the hint of a smile tugging at her lips.

"You girls better have this mess cleaned up before we open," she said, but her voice was playful.

After she'd gone, I turned to Kiri. "So would you mind if I went to the premiere with Cabe? Be honest."

"Are you kidding?" Kiri tossed a wet towel toward me. "Cabe would be miserable without you there. You *better* be his date."

A smile spread across my face, and I clasped my hands together, hopping up and down. "Eeee! I'm going to go to a movie premiere with Cabe Sadler!" Then I froze in panic. "Omigod. I'm going to go to a movie premiere with Cabe Sadler." I started gasping for air.

Kiri slipped her arm around me. "Quit hyperventilating. Maybe we can go shopping later today. Val and Phoebe can come, too. We'll find you a killer dress to wear. You'll look so fabulous that no one will be able to take their eyes off you."

"But . . . maybe I *want* them to take their eyes off me?"

Kiri laughed, then shrugged. "Okay, so we'll find something that says 'I'm fabulous but sh—'" She caught herself before "shy" came out of her mouth.

"Fabulous but . . . demure?" I suggested.

"Demure." Kiri contemplated. "That's sounds very old-school Hollywood. I *love* it! You'll look perfect."

"*Not* perfect," I responded. "I'll look like me."

* * *

I stared out at the red carpet, my stomach fluttering. Hundreds of fans and paparazzi were pushing against the ropes that kept them off the carpet, and there were even some of New York's finest on security detail. Actresses walked the red carpet in to-die-for dresses, waving to the crowd. Above the heads of fans waved a sea of pink and red hearts, homemade by people in the crowd and emblazoned with glittery messages like WE LOVE CABE and BE MY VERY VALENTINE.

I sat back against the leather seat of the limo, suddenly wondering what on earth I'd been thinking when I'd agreed to this.

"Hey," Cabe said beside me. "Are you okay?"

He looked so handsome in his black tuxedo, with its burgundy lapels, that I could barely concentrate on forming any thoughts at all. Finally, I blurted, "What if I trip and fall on my face? What if people yell or throw rotten tomatoes at me?"

Cabe smiled, squeezing my hand. "Are you kidding? If anyone even tried to launch a rotten tomato, I'd dive in front of you and take the hit."

I laughed a little at that, then smoothed out my dress with shaking fingers. "I'm not sure I can do this."

I glanced at Cabe worriedly.

"Okay," he said. He slid his phone out of his pocket and swiped the screen, then held it out to me. "Does that look like a girl who could ever be capable of flubbing a movie premiere?"

I stared at the photo. Mina had taken it back at the house, about half an hour ago. (She was still grounded, so seemed happy to have *something* to do, at least.)

Cabe and I were standing in my kitchen, his arm around me. My hair was swept up in a loose knot at the base of my neck, and wisps of it trailed by my ears, making me look surprisingly sophisticated. My dress, a shade of deep rose, swept across my shoulders in a sweetheart neckline and down my legs in cascading folds adorned with silk flower petals. I was smiling confidently in the photo, looking at the camera like I was brave enough to take on the world.

"There's something else, too," Cabe added. "I was going to save it until after the premiere, but Kiri said I should use it in case of an emergency. I think this qualifies." He tapped the window between us and Ben. Ben rolled the window down and passed a medium-sized pastry box back to Cabe.

Cabe set the box in his lap, then opened the lid. I laughed in delight. Inside was an enormous heart-shaped donut with pink icing and the words, *"To My Very Fine, Very Mine Valentine. Love, Caleb."*

"I think that has to be the sweetest thing anyone's ever done for me," I whispered. "Thank you."

He grinned. "Maybe a little snack will help you find your bravery?" He pinched off a bite for me, then one for himself, and we touched them together in a "cheers" motion before popping them into our mouths.

"Mmmm, delicious," I said. "Kiri might hate donuts, but she sure knows how to bake them."

"Actually, *I* baked this donut," Cabe said shyly. "This afternoon at Doughlicious. Kiri helped a little with writing the words, but I did the rest." He reached for my hand. "Here's the thing. I've been to hundreds of movie premieres. If I have to miss this one, it's no big deal. My manager will be furious, but I can deal with that. If you're not ready, then—"

"No," I interrupted. "I want to do this." And I did. It was important to Cabe. And if we were going to spend time together, I'd have to try to get used to the limelight. Not all the time, but sometimes, for his sake.

"I might not be brave enough to take on the whole world by myself," I said. "But I'm not by myself, am I?" I smiled at him. I had Cabe, and my parents, and Kiri and Mina. And Phoebe and Val and Ms. Feld. So many people who cared about me and who would stand by me, no matter what.

I glanced out the window. "Besides, look who just showed up." I watched Sonora Grace sashaying down the red carpet in a sequin dress, striking poses every few seconds for the cameras. Cabe's manager had invited her to the premiere to help promote *Donut Go Breaking My Heart.* "She'll make sure to steal the spotlight long enough for us to walk in." Cabe laughed as I straightened in my seat and put my hand on the door handle. "Are you ready?"

"Not quite," he said mysteriously. "There's just one more thing I need to do first."

Before I could ask, he took my face in his hands. His mouth met mine in a soft, sweet kiss. I tasted the faintest trace of icing on his lips as everything spun around me, dizzying and exhilarating.

He pulled away gently, and I had to press my hands into the seat to reorient myself to the world again.

"Wow," I managed breathlessly. "Please tell me that wasn't acting."

He smiled. "I could never fake my feelings for you."

He kissed me again. "Now I'm ready," he said finally, and so was I.

Ben opened the door for us. Cabe climbed out, then extended his hand to me. I took one more deep breath, then stepped out of the car and into the flashing lights of hundreds of cameras.

"I've got you, Valentine," Cabe whispered, lifting his elbow so I could slide my arm through his.

And he did, hand *and* heart.

donut
recipes

Craving donuts that will melt your heart? Sheyda
and Cabe fell for these sweet treats and you will,
too! Just remember to always use adult supervision
when you're using a stove top or oven, or when
you're handling hot foods. Bake up a batch for your
own Very Valentine. Mmmm . . . they'll taste
doughlicious!

Caramel Dream Donuts

For the baked vanilla donuts:

1 cup flour

1 tsp. baking powder

¾ cup granulated sugar

½ tsp. cinnamon

½ cup buttermilk

4 tbsp. butter

1 egg

2 tsp. vanilla extract

Preheat your oven to 325 degrees. Spray a nonstick donut pan with cooking spray, or grease it with butter. Combine the flour, baking powder, sugar, and cinnamon in a medium bowl. In a smaller bowl, combine the buttermilk and egg and whisk together. Melt the butter in the micro-wave in a microwave-safe container, then add it to the buttermilk mixture. Stir in the vanilla extract. Pour the buttermilk mixture into the flour mixture and blend well. Pour the batter into the donut pan, making sure to keep the batter just below where the donut hole will be (if you overfill, the batter will bake over the hole). Bake the donuts for approximately ten minutes, then remove from the oven. Let the donuts bake a few more minutes in the pan before trying to remove them to a wire cooling rack. Let the donuts cool. Use the remaining batter to bake a second batch of donuts. Makes 10-12 donuts.

For the caramel icing:

1 cup of light brown sugar

4 tbsp. butter

⅛ cup cream

1 tsp. vanilla extract

¼ cup powdered sugar

1 tube of chocolate cake decorator's icing

Sea salt

For the icing, melt the brown sugar and butter over medium heat in a saucepan on the stove. Add the cream, and let it bubble gently for about five minutes. Slowly add the powdered sugar and let the icing thicken. Don't let it get too thick, though, or dipping the donuts in it may be difficult. Remove from heat and stir in the vanilla extract. Dip the top of each donut into the icing, then place the donut on a wire rack or wax paper. While the caramel icing is still moist, drizzle chocolate icing over the top, and sprinkle with a dash of sea salt. Let the icing set. Enjoy!

Cheesecake Crumble Donuts

For the donuts:

1 cup flour

1 tsp. baking powder

¾ cup granulated sugar

½ cup buttermilk

4 tbsp. butter

1 egg

2 tsp. vanilla extract

Preheat your oven to 325 degrees. Spray a nonstick donut pan with cooking spray, or grease it with butter. Combine the flour, baking powder, and sugar in a medium bowl. In a smaller bowl, combine the buttermilk and egg and whisk together. Melt the butter in the microwave in a microwave-safe container, then add it to the buttermilk mixture. Stir in the vanilla extract. Pour the butter-milk mixture into the flour mixture and blend well. Pour the batter into the donut pan, making sure to keep the batter just below where the donut hole will be (if you over-fill, the batter will bake over the hole). Bake the donuts for approximately ten minutes, then remove from the oven. Let the donuts bake a few more minutes in the pan before trying to remove them to a wire cooling rack. Let the donuts cool. Use the remaining batter to bake a second batch of donuts. Makes 10-12 donuts.

For the cheesecake icing:

1 cup powdered sugar

1 block of cream cheese, softened

½ cup chopped strawberries

½ cup graham cracker crumbs

Pink sprinkles

Milk (optional)

With a hand mixer, beat the powdered sugar and cream cheese together until smooth and creamy. Add in the strawberries and blend. If the icing is very thick, add a teaspoon of milk at a time until it becomes thinner. Dip the top of the each donut into the icing, then place the donut on a wire rack or wax paper. While the glaze is moist, sprinkle the donuts with graham cracker crumbs and pink sprinkles. Let the icing set. Enjoy!

Nutty Professor Donuts

For baked chocolate donuts:

1 cup flour

1 tsp. baking powder

¼ cup unsweetened cocoa powder

¾ cup granulated sugar

4 tbsp. butter

½ cup buttermilk

1 egg

1 tsp. vanilla or almond extract (your choice)

½ cup chocolate chip morsels

Preheat your oven to 325 degrees. Spray a nonstick donut pan with cooking spray, or grease it with butter. Combine the flour, baking powder, cocoa powder, and sugar in a medium bowl. In a smaller bowl, combine the buttermilk and egg and whisk together. Melt the butter in the microwave in a microwave safe container, then add it to the buttermilk mixture. Stir in the vanilla or almond extract, and then the chocolate chips. Pour the buttermilk mixture into the flour mixture and blend well. Pour the batter into the donut pan, making sure to keep the batter just below where the donut hole will be (if you overfill, the batter will bake over the hole). Bake the donuts for approximately ten minutes, then remove from the oven. Let the donuts bake a few more minutes in the pan before trying to remove them to a wire cooling rack. Let the donuts cool. Use the remaining batter to bake a second batch of donuts. Makes 10-12 donuts.

For the peanut butter and honey icing:

½ cup creamy smooth peanut butter

½ cup powdered sugar

⅛ tsp. vanilla extract

2 tbsp. butter

Honey

Almond slivers (optional)

Milk (as needed)

In the microwave, melt the butter in a microwave-safe container. Then heat the peanut butter in the microwave until it softens and thins. Mix the butter and peanut butter together, then blend in the powdered sugar with a hand mixer. Add the vanilla. If the icing is too thick, add a splash of milk to thin it. Dip the top of the each donut into the icing, then place the donut on a wire rack or wax paper. While the icing is still moist, drizzle with zigzags of honey. Finally, sprinkle with almond slivers. Let the icing set. Enjoy!

About the Author

Suzanne Nelson has written several children's books, including *Cake Pop Crush*, *You're Bacon Me Crazy*, *Macarons at Midnight*, *Hot Cocoa Hearts*, and *Serendipity's Footsteps*. She lives with her family in Ridgefield, Connecticut, where she can also be found experimenting with all kinds of cooking. Learn more about Suzanne at www.suzannenelson.com, or follow her on Twitter @snelsonbooks or on Instagram @suzannenelsonbooks.

Don't miss these
delicious reads
by Suzanne Nelson!

glazed
and confused

Sheyda is a behind-the-scenes girl. She loves
helping out in the kitchen of Doughlicious, the donut
shop run by the parents of her best friend, Kiri. And Sheyda loves
designing stage sets while Kiri performs in the spotlight.

Then lights, camera . . . surprise! Tween heartthrob
Cabe Sadler is filming his next movie *in* Doughlicious! Kiri is sure
this will lead to stardom, and perhaps a date with Cabe.
But somehow it's *Sheyda* who gets picked
for a small role in the film.

To make matters worse, Cabe seems spoiled and rude.
Too bad he's so cute. Can Sheyda overcome her stage
fright, get to know the real Cabe, and find

Donut photo © Helena Queen/Thinkstock
Cover design: Jennifer Rinaldi

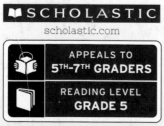

SCHOLASTIC
scholastic.com

APPEALS TO
5TH–7TH GRADERS

READING LEVEL
GRADE 5

More leveling information for this book:
www.scholastic.com/readinglevel

ISBN 978-1-338-04363-1

EAN

9 781338 043631